GW01374482

DAY OF THE VIKINGS

A THRILLER
J.F. PENN

This book is a work of fiction. The characters, incidents and dialogue are drawn from the author's imagination and are not to be construed as real. Any resemblance to actual events or persons, living or dead, is fictionalized or coincidental.

Day of the Vikings
Copyright © J.F.Penn (2014). All rights reserved.
First edition. Printed 2014.

www.JFPenn.com

ISBN: 978-1-912105-40-3

The right of Joanna Penn to be identified as the author of this work has been asserted by the author in accordance with the Copyright, Designs and Patents Act,1988. All rights reserved. No part of this publication may be reproduced, stored in a retrieval system, or transmitted, in any form, or by any means, electronic, mechanical, photocopying, recording or otherwise, without the priorpermission of the publishers.

This book is sold subject to the condition that it shall not, by way of trade or otherwise, be lent, resold, hired out, or otherwise circulated without the author's prior consent in any form of binding or cover other than that in which it is published and without a similar condition being imposed on the subsequent purchaser.

Requests to publish work from this book should be sent to:
joanna@CurlUpPress.com

Cover and Interior Design: JD Smith Design

Printed by Lightning Source

www.CurlUpPress.com

*"Sól tér sortna, sígr fold í mar,
hverfa af himni heiðar stjörnur."*

"The sun turns black, earth sinks in the sea.
The hot stars down from heaven are whirled."

Völuspá, Prophecy of the Seeress,
from the Icelandic Poetic Edda

PROLOGUE

THE NIGHT SKY FLICKERED with shades of green, at first jade and then cerulean, winking through chameleon colors and morphing into pink. Spears of silver lanced from the heavens, as if stars rained down onto the earth. The aurora borealis filled the expanse of the sky with unnatural hues illuminating the faces below.

"The armor of the Valkyries blesses this sacrifice," a woman's voice called out, low and commanding. "The gods have sent the solar winds to herald our new dawn."

Shades of indigo and turquoise enlivened the Merry Dancers, as the aurora was known on the Orkney Islands in the far north of Scotland, closer to Norway than London. Here the people still lived close to the ocean and the sky, understanding the power of the wind to sweep away the past and bring renewal again.

The lights touched the face of the man bound to one of the standing stones, his eyes glazed. He smiled with rapture as he saw the spirits leap and caper in the vault of heaven.

The Ring of Brodgar, a Neolithic stone circle thousands of years old, stood at the center of a natural cauldron shaped by the surrounding hills. The prehistoric ritual complex was the focal point for the energies that lay beneath this ancient land. On this night, it bore witness to the renewal of vows not spoken for hundreds of years.

There were seven men in the ring, dressed in furs, who knelt before one woman. Her hair was long and gray with one bright blue streak, blowing in the high winds to fly up around her like a nimbus of power. She was the Crone, embodiment of wisdom, though none dare call her that to her face. Her fingers clutched a wooden staff carved with runes. She stamped it onto the earth as she approached the bound man.

"A storm is coming," she proclaimed.

"A storm is coming," the men around her echoed, falling to their knees. They began to chant, a low rumbling repetition more animal than human, a tongue not spoken for centuries in these parts, and feared when it was.

The woman pulled a knife from her leather belt as she called to the skies.

"Odin, All-Father, give me your wisdom, lend me your prophecy, that tonight we can see the path to restoration." She touched the tip of the knife to the man's chest, gentle at first, but then she pressed into his skin, drawing rune lines across his flesh as blood rose in the path of the blade. "*Fylliz fiorvi feigra manna, rýðr ragna siot rauðom dreyra.*" The man uttered a moan, flinging his head back against the stone. The woman kept the blade moving, tracing the rune lines that emerged like a dread tattoo on his skin. "It sates itself on the life-blood of fated men, paints red the powers' homes with crimson gore."

Her voice echoed with the voices of those who had worshipped under the same skies for millennia. On the last word, the woman reversed the knife so the hooked part of the blade was uppermost. With strength that seemed beyond her, she thrust the knife into the man's lower belly, wrenching it up and around. The man howled, a sound of wolves and wild things that once had stalked this land. The stink of entrails filled the air as intestines oozed out, dripping with blood, and the man's cries resounded amongst the stones.

"Accept this sacrifice, Odin, god of Death." The woman's voice was husky now, as if she spoke to a lover. "Take this life as our payment for your hidden knowledge."

She turned to one of the kneeling men and he handed her a simple iron cup. Holding the knife, the woman slashed at the throat of the victim, opening his neck and silencing his howls. Blood spurted out over her and she leaned in to receive the blessing of the giver. She held the cup to the open wound, letting blood pulse into the chalice as the life force left the man and he sagged against his bonds.

"Give us your wisdom," the woman whispered as she mixed in the juice of the deadly mushrooms from a vial. Only the right measure would bring the visions, a glimpse of the other side. Too much and they would die here in shaking fits and voided bodies. She took a long sip, blood staining her mouth, and then passed it to the first man kneeling before her.

The woman's eyes flickered as the warm blood trickled down her throat and the drug began to work in her. She looked up at the aurora above the standing stones, the glory of the heavens. Surely it was Asgard, home of the gods, revealed through the portal of the firmament above. The branches of Yggdrasil, the world tree, entwined their realms together, its leaves made from the sinews of warriors who perished with the name of Odin on their lips. Too long had she waited, her patience tested by the gods, but now it was finally time.

The cawing of ravens began as a far-off sound but then a host of them flew across the sky, highlighted by the colors of the aurora. They circled the group below, their shrieking filling the stone circle, almost blocking the eerie light. It seemed like a thousand thousand of them thronged the skies, their cries a paean to the All-Father, a blessing on their acts in His name. The men on their knees were transfixed by the whirling birds, their black feathers shining with the hues of the bright sky, at once emerald green and then slashed with bright vermilion.

"Odin the Raven God is come to us," the woman cried out, her hands raised toward the winged messengers, blood still staining her flesh. "Here are Huginn and Muninn, thought and mind, the ravens that Odin sends out to search for knowledge. Here is our sign, and now is the time. We will go south and retrieve that which will bring us power again."

CHAPTER 1

MORGAN SIERRA WALKED THROUGH the grand Neo-Classical entrance of the British Museum into the Great Court. The early morning sun filtered through the paneled glass ceiling high above, casting lined shadows onto the cool stone beneath her feet. Morgan couldn't help but smile to be here again, a place of magic for anyone as obsessed with seeking knowledge as she was. Part of her wanted to turn right toward the Enlightenment Gallery, where every object was a gateway to another rabbit hole of research. Coming here had once been for pleasure only, but now this kind of research was part of her job at the Arcane Religious Knowledge And Numinous Experience Institute, known as ARKANE – the world's most advanced and secret research center for investigating supernatural mysteries.

For a moment, a shadow crossed her face. The last time she had been here, the main exhibition had been religious relics, the blood and bone of saints, sponsored by a man she had later seen turn into a demon in the bone church of Sedlec. Morgan's hand rose to her left side, where the scar he had carved still throbbed in the cold of morning. She shook her head, casting aside the memories. Every mission with ARKANE had its own blend of violence and mystery, and Morgan had accepted both as part of her new life.

After Budapest, she had asked for some time to investigate a book that had been sent to her from Spain, the address label in her father's handwriting although he had been killed by suicide bombers years ago. The impossible package was on her mind now, but Director Marietti had deemed this more urgent, and she had been sent to investigate an artifact on loan to the museum from a private collection of Viking ritual objects. With Morgan's background in the psychology of religion, Marietti thought she would be ideally placed to assess whether ARKANE should send a replica back to the exhibition so they could study the actual artifact privately in the secret vaults below Trafalgar Square.

"Dr. Sierra?"

Morgan turned toward the voice.

"Good morning. The curator sends his apologies, but he's preparing for a big tour. I'm Blake Daniel, another researcher here. He's briefed me on your request, so I'll be taking you through to see it."

Morgan hid her surprise at his appearance with a smile of welcome. With coffee skin and piercing blue eyes, a number-one buzz cut and designer stubble, Blake looked as if he had just come from the set of a music video, not the dusty corridors of the museum. A fleeting thought crossed her mind that she wouldn't say no to a drink with him either. Blake held out a hand and Morgan noticed his gloves, a light coffee color that ensured they didn't stand out too much against his darker skin. It struck her as strange nonetheless to be wearing them indoors on a day that was already warming up. She shook his hand, wondering why he wore them.

"So, tell me about the ARKANE Institute," Blake said, as he led the way around the Great Court toward the Sainsbury Wing where the special Viking exhibition was being held. "It must have some clout considering how fast your request to see the exhibit was processed."

"The Institute is mainly a group of academics working as

a collective. We publish academic articles and run seminars, primarily around religious artifacts and unusual findings."

And then there's the rest of it, Morgan thought. The secret side of ARKANE, with agents working on supernatural mysteries around the world, generally at the flash points of religion and the occult. The ARKANE that held relics and sacred objects of power in the vaults deep under Trafalgar Square. The ARKANE where agents died to keep the rest of the world safe from things that most wouldn't even believe possible. The ARKANE that had threatened her family, and still woke Morgan with nightmares of flames and blood.

Blake turned into the Egyptian hall, where they walked past the Rosetta Stone and gigantic heads of the pharaohs. Every step within the British Museum was packed with treasures that alone would be wondrous, but here were dwarfed by the sheer volume of history. It was a place to be lost in wonder for days, and Morgan was fleetingly jealous of Blake for working here.

"So, what's your particular interest in the staff of Skara Brae?" Blake asked. "It's not exactly the focal point of the exhibition. In fact, it's more of a sideshow."

Morgan smiled, for the rabbit hole of intellectual curiosity was her own addiction and anyone who worked in the museum would understand her fascinations.

"I found an obscure reference in the Icelandic *Konungsbók*," she said. "It tells of a year in which floods would rise and the aurora borealis would be seen in southern lands; when the blood of a *völva*, a shamanic seeress skilled in illusion, would awaken the demons of old and they would usher in the final winters, heralding Ragnarok."

"That's the Viking apocalypse myth, right?" Blake asked, as he led the way through the galleries. "The fabled fall of the gods, when the final battle between all races will bring the giant sea serpent from the ocean and would lead to the world being submerged in water."

Morgan nodded, pleased to find someone so well-versed in the lore. "Of course, Britain has experienced record flooding this year and the aurora was seen in the most southerly parts of the country. Very unusual. As I delved further into the prophecy, I discovered the staff of Skara Brae which has an unusual rune. I wanted to see it for myself, rather than just in photographs, and this seemed like a good chance to examine it."

Blake pulled open a double door, waving his hand to indicate she should enter first.

"This is the back door to the exhibition, as I presume you want to skip the preliminaries. The coins, gold and jewelry are nothing to what's in the main hall, and I've put the staff in a side room so we won't be disturbed when the exhibition opens up to the public." He checked his watch. "We'd better get moving actually, as the first visitors will be in soon. The Vikings seem to be quite the popular thing these days. We're sold out daily."

The main exhibition hall was huge, dominated by the remains of a Viking longship found in Roskilde, Denmark. Ancient spars formed part of the vessel, held in shape by a metal frame with open ribs to see inside. Even with its skeletal appearance, the sheer magnitude of the ship was impressive. Glass cases and information boards surrounded the central focus on all sides, but the boat was clearly the highlight of the exhibition.

"I think more people are coming to see this than your staff," Blake said. "Although we do have some rather good swords, as well." He gestured to a glass case containing longswords and metal axe heads. The clinical display didn't do much for the imagination, but Morgan knew the damage a blade could do on a human body. Her scar throbbed at the memory. "We even have a Neo-Viking group coming today," Blake continued.

"Neo-Viking?" Morgan asked, turning away from the

sword case.

"Yes, apparently it's all the rage at the moment. Something to do with the popularity of *Game of Thrones* and how much it's influenced by Norse mythology. Of course, we Brits have always liked dressing up and doing pitched battles for tourists at castles." Blake grinned. "This is just another iteration on the theme. The group will be in later, so we might catch a glimpse of them. The curator is excited by their enthusiasm – there are some impressive beards, according to their website."

Blake raised an eyebrow, and Morgan couldn't help but smile at the thought of what a band of Neo-Vikings might look like. She turned to look into another display case. At sight of what it contained, the smile died on her lips. A metal conical helmet sat above a Viking jawbone, the teeth still intact in a macabre grimace. These men were not to be ridiculed.

"They filed their teeth," Blake said. "And colored the grooves between them, as well as tattooing their skin to intimidate those they set to plunder."

Morgan imagined a longboat the size of this hall filled with warriors of this ferocity, and her hands itched for a weapon. She had once vowed to leave physical violence aside, after the death of her husband Elian in a hail of bullets on the Golan Heights. She left the Israeli Defense Force for academia, but ARKANE had thrown her back into the fray. These days she understood that the adrenalin rush of the fight was just as much a part of her as her intellectual curiosity, and she was slowly beginning to accept her shadow self.

Blake pushed open a door at the back of the exhibition hall and led Morgan into a small room.

"Here it is: the staff of Skara Brae. There are two other staffs, as well, which we've left in the case out in the main exhibition hall."

The staff lay on a white table with a pair of white gloves

next to it for careful handling. Not that she'd be able to do any damage to it, Morgan thought, for the staff was iron and well made. The top was thicker than the rest, designed with a woven pattern, representing the threads of fate that could be controlled through spinning or entwining, or cutting and burning.

"You can see the inscription here," Morgan said, pointing at the rune carved in the middle of the staff. It was a geometric pattern of lines and curves and cross-hatches. "It's called ægishjálmr, the helm of awe, which Vikings believed had the power to invoke illusions and fear through incantation and inscription. This staff is the only example of its kind found in the world with this rune. The *völva,* or seeress, who held this would have been considered powerful enough to span the nine worlds of the Viking Yggdrasil."

The word *völva* meant 'staff bearer,' and they practiced *seidh*, a sorcery that bound the natural world to that of the gods. These women were powerful, with the ability to read and write runes, casting their will upon the world. Morgan had discovered that most of the staffs and swords found in graves had been bent or rolled, ritually 'killed' when the owner died. It was said that this made the powers disappear, that they were lost into the earth. But this staff hadn't been bent, or rolled. It was pristine. Did that mean it could still be wielded by those who knew the rites? Once, Morgan would have laughed at the idea, but the things she had seen in the fires of Pentecost, the bone church of Sedlec and the Egyptian temple of Abu Simbel had opened her eyes. This physical world was not all there was, and only those with eyes that could see beyond knew the truth.

Morgan put on the gloves and picked up the staff, its iron weight heavy in her hands. It had the heft of a poker kept by an open fire to prod the coals, a practical object, not something ethereal like an imagined fantasy wand. In her years of practicing Krav Maga, the Israeli martial art, Morgan had used pieces of metal like this as weapons many times. Used as a club, this could surely kill, but was it more than a lump of metal? Were its properties even something that could be empirically studied in the ARKANE labs? She laid the staff down again and bent closer to examine the rune.

CHAPTER 2

BLAKE WATCHED AS MORGAN leaned closer to the staff, brushing a long dark curl from around her face. Her eyes were cobalt blue with a slash of violet in the right eye that made Blake want to learn what else was unusual about Dr. Sierra. He had read up on the official side of ARKANE, but Morgan was not what he had expected from a purely academic research institute, and he had his suspicions about what else they might be involved in. Morgan was toned muscle under her slight curves, and she moved with the grace of someone acutely aware of her surroundings – the type of vigilance he would expect of someone in the military. There was some kind of accent in her words, a hint of Israeli perhaps, and she looked to be Mediterranean in origin. With a name like Sierra, Spain would be the obvious choice.

His own mixed heritage made the cultural guessing game a regular pastime for Blake. His blue eyes were from his Swedish father, and his darker skin tone from his Nigerian mother. He would have an Afro if he let his hair grow any longer, but he preferred the razor buzz cut. London was the perfect place to people watch and guess where they had traveled from, or perhaps where their great grandparents had originated. This was a true multicultural city, and one that embraced the stranger, since all were outsiders in some form. This was the Britain he loved and belonged to, the endless meshing of culture in the river of city life.

"Do you have any more information on the grave it came from?" Morgan asked, standing up straight. "Or if other grave objects were found with it?"

Blake shook his head. "The curator said that little is known about the staff, which is why he was happy for me to show it to you. Believe me, if he had known anymore, he would have scheduled several hours to talk to you himself."

A flicker of dangerous thought surfaced in Blake's mind as he spoke. He usually preferred to keep quiet about it, but he had an unusual gift that could perhaps help Morgan in her quest for knowledge. Some called it clairvoyance, others psychometry. In his darkest moments, Blake knew it for the curse that it was. Whatever its name, Blake could read objects through their emotional resonance. The gloves he wore protected him from accidental contact, but they also covered a patchwork of ivory scars, where his religious father had tried to beat the visions from him.

A babble of voices came from the main exhibition room, breaking their quiet study. Blake could hear the curator speaking loudly, his excitement at sharing his work causing his words to run into one another.

"The ship was built after 1025 AD and from stem to stern it's thirty-six meters, which makes it the longest Viking ship ever discovered. We have calculated that there would have been thirty-nine pairs of oars, with seventy-eight rowers to serve them."

Blake couldn't help smiling at how bored the group must be with all the facts and figures, but it wasn't often that the curator got to hold forth to so many. Most people just wanted to see the longswords, and the bones of the decapitated Vikings held in the central exhibit, clearly the result of a massacre. British pride perhaps, fighting back against the widely held belief that Vikings raped and plundered with no defiance from the local population.

Morgan was still examining the iron staff, so Blake pulled open the side door a crack, trying to catch a glimpse of the Neo-Viking group that the curator was escorting. There were several groups of other tourists in the exhibition hall, but the Neo-Vikings weren't hard to spot. There were five men wearing rough-spun tunics over long trousers, wrapped round the middle with leather belts. They had fur skins over their shoulders, real ones by the look of them. Their faces were expressionless, even as they were shown the case of the Norse helmet and jawbone. One of the men wore a close-fitting tunic that revealed muscular arms, his left bicep tattooed with a raven in flight, its feathers entwined with rune letters. The man's eyes darted around the room, taking in everyone's position. He seemed strangely dissociated with what they were supposedly here to view.

The group shifted as they moved to the next case, revealing a woman in their midst. She could have been anywhere between fifty and seventy, her features wrinkled but her skin glowing with an inner radiance. Her dark eyes were sharply focused on the curator, as if sucking his words into a bottomless pool. Her long gray hair was wound into a plait that hung down her back, with one blue streak that ran through it like the lapis lazuli jewelry held in the Egyptian rooms next door.

"The Neo-Vikings are here," Blake said, turning back to Morgan with a smile. "They look pretty convincing, actually."

She looked up at him just as an explosion shook the building and the high-pitched shriek of the emergency alarms filled the air.

CHAPTER 3

THE EXPLOSION WAS COMPLETELY unexpected in this hall of ancient knowledge, but Morgan's military training kicked in and she pulled Blake to the floor, under the protection of the broad table while the alarm shrieked around them. In these old buildings, the threat of falling plaster and stone could be worse than any initial damage. Part of her expected more explosions.

"I've got to go and help with the evacuation," Blake shouted above the wail of the alarm and the screaming voices from the exhibition hall. "We've got to get everyone out of here."

He tried to get up, but Morgan pulled him back down.

"Wait," she said. "In Israel, this kind of thing is part of our daily drill. You don't run yet, because you could be running into something worse."

Her mind flashed to her days in the IDF: the bomb attacks she had experienced, the soldiers she had treated for PTSD … her father's body blown apart by a suicide bomber, a sack of oranges spilled on the road amongst severed limbs.

There was something very wrong here. She checked her phone – no reception. Then she heard it. In between the rhythmic siren noise, it was quiet. The screams had been silenced.

"Listen," she whispered. "Next door."

Blake cocked his head sideways. "Maybe the people have been evacuated?"

"Stay there. I'm going to have a look."

Morgan scooted out from under the table and went to the door, pulling it open a tiny crack as Blake had done minutes before.

People lay on the floor, hands on their heads, while around the room, the Neo-Vikings stood with handguns drawn. The alarm suddenly stopped and the sound of smashing glass filled the room. There was a gasp from the floor.

"You can't!"

A cry of pain followed as one of the men kicked the curator into silence.

Across the room, Morgan saw an older woman reach into a glass case. She lifted out one of the iron staffs and examined the surface before flinging it to the floor. The crash brought another collective gasp from the hostages. The woman took out the second staff, examining it with jerky movements, like an addict desperate for a fix.

"Where is it?" she said, quietly at first, her voice a Scottish lilt. "Where is the real staff?"

The woman spun around and Morgan saw burning fury in her eyes, her hands clenched into claws.

"Bring the curator here."

As two of the big men dragged the curator from the floor, Morgan knew she only had seconds to make a decision. The woman wanted the staff of Skara Brae, but once she had it, what would she be able to do with it? Not so long ago, Morgan would have given up the lump of iron with no question. She would save these people from harm and the witch would leave with her staff. But Morgan's perception of the world had changed after what she had seen with ARKANE. Sometimes darker things were at stake.

The men pushed the curator to his knees before the woman.

"The staff of power isn't here," she whispered. "Where is it?"

"How dare you come in here and threaten these people!" the curator blustered, straightening his spine, words infused with the pride of the British Empire. "This is the British Museum, a place for everybody to see these wonders, not your private shopping center."

Morgan's heart thumped in her chest at his foolhardy words. Couldn't he see the intent in the old woman's eyes? Could he only see a group he had laughed at with his colleagues this morning? With her military training, Morgan could probably stop some initial harm coming to the man, but there were too many of the Neo-Vikings and no backup. She was powerless to stop whatever might happen. She felt movement behind her and breath on her neck. Blake was at her side, watching through the gap over her shoulder. Adrenalin surging and senses heightened, Morgan felt the heat of him standing close to her, and smelled a hint of clean soap on his skin.

The old woman laughed and then began to chant, her voice morphing into that of the *völva*, the shamanic priestess. Her fingers wove in the air, spinning and dancing, as she spoke words of power that had long lay dormant. The Neo-Viking men looked at the floor as if scared to watch, but the others in the room were captivated, staring at the woman. She looked mad, unhinged. Then, the rattle of bones filled the air and a gasp of horror rippled around the room.

From the pit of the slaughtered Vikings, the bones rose into the air, disjointed skeletons spinning above the hollow Viking ship, beginning to knit back together before their eyes. Morgan heard Blake's sharp intake of breath next to her ear.

"I am the Valkyrie," the woman said. "I am the Corpse

Goddess who decides who lives and who dies, who comes to feast in Valhalla until Ragnarok."

Some of the skeletons were missing heads, but they began to move in the air regardless, flexing bony joints, as if just waking up. Morgan blinked and rubbed her eyes. Part of her understood that the priestesses were fabled experts of illusion, but she could smell the decay; she could see the hacked ends of the men's fingers, where they had tried to defend themselves against the slaughter so long ago.

"Your security has been overpowered," the Valkyrie said. "All visitors and employees have been evacuated except for you, and my men will be spreading out through the museum. You're all my hostages until I get that staff. Give it to me now, old man, and perhaps I won't release the *einherjar* amongst you all."

The curator's eyes widened at this, and Morgan remembered from her research that the *einherjar* were a band of warriors who had died in battle and awaited the day of Ragnarok to herald the final war cry. Were these skeletal figures truly the vanguard of the woman's ghostly army, or was it all just illusion?

Morgan pushed the door shut. There was no time to wait any longer. The curator would give them up any second.

"We have to go now," she whispered, grabbing the staff from the table. "They want this and I'm afraid if we give it to them, things will get a whole lot worse."

Blake's face was a mask of confusion and wonder. Morgan saw the flicker of indecision in his eyes before he seemed to settle on trusting her.

"The emergency exit leads out to the back of the building onto Montague Place," he said, pushing the exit door. "This way."

They walked quickly away from the room to another door that led out to a main exit. Morgan pushed the door slightly and peeked through the gap. One of the Neo-Vikings stood guard there, one hand on the pommel of a broadsword and the other holding a gun.

Morgan pushed the door closed again. "We can't get out this way."

"Then we have to go up and over, across to the exits on the other side of the building," Blake whispered.

The crash of a slamming door echoed through the corridor, followed by a roar of disappointment.

"Find them!" The Valkyrie's words were followed by several sets of footsteps heading in their direction.

"This way," Blake said, running up a staircase on light feet. Morgan ran after him, past mosaics from Halicarnassus and Carthage, the once-bright colors now dull with age. There were spiraling vines, dolphins leaping through the waves and Roman nobles feasting, crowned with laurel wreaths. Celebrate, Morgan thought, for tomorrow we die.

At the top of the stairs they turned into the upper galleries, where Egyptian death and afterlife were displayed and explained. The dead were bound in linen and laid in wooden cases, the inner caskets painted with the gods and symbols of prosperity in the everlasting. Their skin was burnished leather, features shrunken but still visible, even down to perfectly preserved eyelashes. Morgan shuddered. Skeletons were one thing, but she didn't want these bodies coming to a semblance of life again.

The heavy footsteps were almost behind them now. There was no way they would get out without being caught.

"Down," Morgan said, pushing Blake behind one of the display cases so he wouldn't be seen. She spun around to stand just inside the door to the next room, next to an exhibit of *shabti* figures – servants for the afterlife in blue-glazed faience and serpentine. She held the iron staff high like a baseball bat ready to strike. If the old witch wanted it for death, maybe they should start with some of her own men.

The adrenalin pumped now and Morgan's heart pounded.

Once upon a time she had called it fear, but her years in the IDF had trained that out of her. Now, she called it anticipation. She itched to hit something, craving the rush that only violence could soothe. Life was simple when it came down to survival; movement into battle felt like a meditation. In a flash, she understood why the Vikings had roamed the world, raiding and exploring new places, and why perhaps these men craved the same existence.

A footstep came from just outside the doorway. As the first man walked through, Morgan swung the iron staff at his face, aiming behind his head. He leaned back in reaction, but the metal bar slammed into his nose anyway, the crunch of bone resounding in the empty hall. The man reeled, clutching his face, blood streaming through his fingers as he fell to his knees groaning.

A second Neo-Viking stood behind him, over six foot, a meaty man with piggy eyes who squinted at the staff as if he could barely see it.

"You defile the sacred," he rasped. "Give it to me, bitch, and I may let you live."

Morgan stood to face him, slamming the iron staff into her opposite palm. She smiled, her eyes cold.

"Come and get it."

CHAPTER 4

As the man lunged for her, Morgan stepped back and used the staff to smash the exhibition case next to her, sending shards of glass flying. Momentarily blinded, he raised his hands to his face. Morgan used the rounded end of the staff to thrust at his throat with a lightning-fast movement. She forced herself to hold back at the last moment, with the realization that she didn't want to kill the man, only leave him incapacitated.

The man's face was a mix of surprise and terror, his eyes wide. He gasped for breath, one hand clutching at the broken edges of the display case, blood staining the ancient artifacts. His throat was already visibly swelling and bruising. Morgan waited with the staff raised, ready to knock him down, but he slumped to the floor, chest heaving as he tried to draw breath. The other man still clutched his broken nose, moaning against the wall in the other room. The edges of her rage bubbled, the righteous anger that emerged when she or those she loved were threatened. But she was learning to hold it back, and these men weren't the true enemy.

Blake stepped out warily from behind the display case.

"You're no academic, Dr. Sierra." His voice had an edge of respect and a whole lot of curiosity in it.

"And these are no Viking warriors," Morgan said, considering the men on the ground. "This should have been harder. But we should move, in case they send backup. These guys will be up and about, wanting some retribution soon enough."

"This way." Blake hurried off down the gallery, turning several times, past bearded warriors in sculptures from Mesopotamia and artifacts from the walls of Babylon. Morgan couldn't help but look into the cases as they passed, glimpses of cuneiform engraved on tablets documenting the lives of those thousands of years ago. The academic in her wanted to look closer, but she would have to linger another time. Blake pulled out a bunch of keys as they approached a gallery that was closed for maintenance.

"We can go through here, and I'll lock it behind us. Might hold them off for a while when the next lot come looking. There's an archive storeroom that we can at least stop to think in."

On the other side of the door, Morgan followed Blake through another gallery and up a little staircase to a door with multiple locks. She raised an eyebrow at the additional security while Blake fiddled with his keys, looking for the right ones.

"I got the keys a few months ago from one of the curators. It's a great place to come and think when I need some space."

***

Blake pushed open the door to the musty room, an archive of some of the less popular exhibits. Or those that they don't want people to know about, Blake thought. He came here for silence and solitude, but also to read in private. Not books, but the objects themselves, losing himself in a world of past lives as a way to bring his own research alive. There were some who commented that his research papers were too fanciful, too full of character and possible scenarios for the objects he studied, but the grant money kept coming, so no one questioned his methods. So far, he had managed to keep his gift almost secret.

"They'll struggle to find us here," Blake said. "This room isn't even on the plans."

"It will be good to stop for a minute." Morgan looked down at her phone, frowning in frustration. "Damn. There's still no reception. They must have a signal jammer for the whole building."

"The evacuation and alarms would have tipped off the police, so I'm sure there's a host of emergency services and reporters outside." He paused. "But you want ARKANE, right? Can they do something more than the police?"

Morgan sighed. "There's more to ARKANE than just academics and conferences."

"I got that from your ability to wield a metal club back there," Blake grinned. "Most impressive. And to be honest, I'm far more interested in what ARKANE does now. Can you tell me anything about it?"

Morgan went silent for a moment, her eyes focusing on a faraway point. She shook her head.

"Not much, sorry. Only that we investigate supernatural mysteries, many of them around religious or cult objects like this one." She held up the staff. "Most of what I'm involved in, you would struggle to believe."

"Is it harder to believe that a Neo-Viking priestess caused long-dead bones to spin in the air, calling warriors from their Valhalla feast?"

Morgan smiled. "Fair point. When I identified this staff as something to be looked into further, I had no idea that others would be seeking it, too. It seems this Valkyrie priestess could possibly wield its power, whereas I can only use it as a blunt club. We need to know more about it."

Blake's heart thumped as he summoned the strength to

speak of that which he kept secret. He rubbed his gloved hands together, the bumps of the scars familiar lines through the fabric. Part of him wanted to wait and see what Morgan would come up with, as he was sure she would get them out of here. But another part wanted to read the staff, a curiosity that made his hands tingle in anticipation.

He pulled the gloves off, revealing his scarred hands, the cinnamon skin marred with criss-crossed ropes of ivory.

"Oh Blake, I'm so sorry," Morgan said, her eyes widening as she took in his extensive injuries.

"My father tried to beat the gift out of me," he said. "He tried to bleed it from my skin, but it always came back."

"What gift?" The violet slash in Morgan's right eye seemed to darken to indigo as she focused on his words. Blake could see no judgment there, only sincere interest.

"I can read objects," he said, although it was hard to put into words the maelstrom of vision that consumed him when he read. "Some call it psychometry, or a form of clairvoyance. Whatever you want to call it, when I touch an object, I can enter into its emotional history. I can see the people and places it touched and feel the emotions that surrounded it. Sometimes it's hazy, but the strongest emotions also bring the most powerful visions."

"So you see violence and murder more often than happiness?"

Blake nodded. "Exactly." That was the curse, along with the flashbacks he experienced of what he witnessed. He drowned his nightmares in tequila most nights, but Morgan didn't need to know about his nocturnal vice. "I've helped the police on a couple of cases, not that they would admit that to anyone, but that has helped me reframe the gift as useful at least." Blake thought of Detective Jamie Brooke and what he had seen of the murder at the Hunterian – the grotesque specimens in jars that revealed the heart of the crime. "Perhaps if I read the staff, we might find out something more about why the Neo-Vikings want it?"

Morgan hesitated. Blake saw uncertainty in her eyes, but only for a second. She held out the staff.

"What can I do to help?"

"Can you just put it down here on the floor?" Blake sat down cross-legged. Morgan put the staff in front of him, sitting down opposite him. Her proximity made him uneasy, aware that she would be watching him, assessing what he was doing. But apparently she had seen stranger things, and to be honest, he was interested to see what was so special about this staff.

"So, how does this work?" Morgan asked. "Do you go into some kind of trance state?"

"I guess you could say that, but if you remove my hands from the staff, I'll come out of it. Sometimes I go pretty deep, and can have physical reactions to what I'm experiencing. If you're worried, just pull the staff away."

Blake laid his hands on the iron rod and closed his eyes, sensing the waves of past experience waiting to wash over him. He dreaded this moment, but also craved it. For as much as he drank to oblivion to forget some of the things he had seen, he also experienced moments of beauty that stood out like diamond stars in the night sky, a precious glimpse into the lives of those long dead.

The veil of consciousness shifted, and Blake reached back with his mind. There was a long period of dark, dormant power that throbbed and hummed, perhaps the time in the grave where the staff had been found. He heard his own pulse before it morphed into the beating of drums and his vision began to clear.

***

They came from the sea in longboats filled with men in heat for battle, the staff of Skara Brae at their head, clutched in the hands of the only woman with them, the *völva* seeress. She wasn't like the women they had left behind, those who served and bore children, subject to their menfolk. There was power in this one – a sense that she was at one with the ferocity of nature, and her will drove the men who followed her, even into death. The drums beat faster as the boats landed on the shore of an island. A priory loomed above them, carved into the rocks, its arches built to the glory of the God these monks served. The green hill slopes wound up to the priory, and the figures of people running could be seen, trying to escape the oncoming raiders.

Blake sensed the excitement of the Viking horde, their blood calling for plunder and slaughter, but under it all a resonance of pure joy. It was the first time he had truly felt it when reading. These men knew happiness in these moments. Perhaps this is what men are truly made for, Blake thought, as the rumble of the drums filled him.

"*Fyllisk fjörvi feigra manna, rýðr ragna sjöt rauðum dreyra.*"

The men shouted Norse words as they spilled out of the boats, their voices a rough chant, evoking the frenzy and hunger of the god Odin as they charged. They called for the gods to feed on the flesh of the dead, and redden this land with gore.

"*Skeggjöld, skálmöld, vindöld, vargöld*," they chanted as they ran. "Axe-time, sword-time, wind-time, wolf-time."

Many were tattooed with the beasts that would stand with them in spirit during battle, and some wore wolf-skin pelts, the heads with teeth bared, adding to the ferocity of their appearance. With longswords and great axes held high, they ran in packs for the villages at the base of the priory, but Blake lost sight of them as he could only remain with the staff. He could hear the screams though, the wailing that soon filled the air, of women raped and men murdered, the village plundered as they died.

The seeress made for the inner rooms of the priory, and her focus thrummed through Blake's core. She wanted something from here, something very specific. He could sense her seeking it out. Two huge men flanked her, swords drawn. They pushed through the heavy wooden double doors into the sanctuary of the priory chapel, where a group of monks huddled near the altar, protecting the relics of the saint. One of them broke away carrying a heavy book, with two others flanking him. The Vikings ignored the group, for there was so much gold here, in the chalices and reliquaries, the wealth of a church that had not yet gone through the pains of the Reformation. The Viking guards stepped forward to begin piling it up for plunder.

One reached for a candlestick topped with an ornate carved eagle as a monk rushed toward them, hands raised in supplication.

"Stop," he cried. "This is the Lord's house."

The Viking backhanded him casually, swatting the man to the floor.

"The punishment of God has come upon us," the monk cried, rising to his knees, hands raised in worship. "Forgive …"

His words were silenced by the thrust of a longsword, the tip of the blade emerging through his back, dripping with blood. The monk's eyes reflected surprise as they glazed over, his mouth open in his last prayer. The Viking withdrew the sword and wiped it on the monk's habit before sheathing it again, turning his attention back to the gold.

"I want the bones of the saint and one of you for my sacrifice to Odin," the seeress said, in the local tongue. "If you give me that now, along with gold for my men, the rest of you will live to rebuild your community. Otherwise, you all die."

CHAPTER 5

BLAKE WATCHED AS THE monks stood in mute silence for a moment, and then one whispered. The others turned. There was a flurry of gesticulation and heated argument. The eldest monk finally stepped forward, his steps faltering, his blue eyes misty with age or the fear of what was to come.

"Take me, but let my brothers leave. I will go soon to meet the Lord anyway."

The seeress nodded, and the other monks hurried away, only one looking back at the brother they had left behind, regret and shame on his face.

"Make it quick, I beg of you," the old monk said, using one of the altar rails to lower himself down, beginning to pray.

"I can't give you that, old man, but perhaps your own god will hear your screams and your place in paradise will be assured." She gestured to the two Viking guards. "Hold him."

The monk struggled as they forced him to bend forward, his back to the *völva*, his prayers spoken in halting Latin, interspersed with panicked breath.

"Sed et si ambulavero in valle mortis non timebo …"

One of the Vikings ripped the monk's habit, pulling it down to reveal thin, sagging skin on old bones. Tucking the staff into her belt, the seeress withdrew a long knife, its blade wickedly sharp with serrated edges.

"… malum quoniam tu mecum es virga tua … et baculus tuus ipsa consolabuntur me."

With surprising strength, she thrust the knife into the monk's back and began to wrench it up and down. The man screamed and writhed, but the Vikings held him as the seeress continued cutting, sawing his ribs away from his spine. Blake felt the pulse of the monk's blood, his agony like a wave. He recoiled from the scene, sinking toward darkness into the tunnel that led back to the present day. The vision of the monk faded and his screams became little more than a whisper. But Blake knew he needed to know more, he had to see what came next in order to understand why the staff was so important. He pushed back along the tug of the staff, and emerged again into the chapel.

The stink of blood and feces filled the air, sweat and fear overlaying them. The monk's body was laid on the floor by the altar now, his ribs splayed out from his spine revealing a bloody cavity where the seeress pulled his viscera out. Blood covered her hands, her fingers curled into talons with fingernails stained crimson.

"Get me a bone from the relic of their saint," she rasped, her voice almost bestial. One of the Vikings went to the altar and opened the reliquary of St Cuthbert, taking the small finger bones out.

The seeress laid the bones on the floor, squatting next to them and crushing them with the blunt end of the staff. She scattered the powder and slivers of bone over the bloody corpse of the monk, muttering words as she waved the iron staff over it. On the final word, she thrust the staff into the raw cavity of the still-steaming body, coating the iron with gore and clots of blood. She stood again and lifted the dripping staff toward the heavens, calling in a language that resonated with power.

"Great Odin, All-Father, give me your vision."

Her eyes rolled back in her head, showing the whites, and she began to convulse. The whole chapel began to shake. The Viking men held onto the walls as the vibrations grew stronger. A great crack filled the air and the flagstones ruptured beneath their feet, steam pouring out and engulfing the seeress in its hot breath. Blake felt the heat in her transmuted through the staff, but she screamed in ecstasy, not pain, as the visions filled her.

"*Alt veit ek, Óðinn! hvar þú auga falt: í inum mæra Mímis brunni,*" she chanted, her eyes opening wider as she spoke, as if surprised by the words that came out of her mouth.

Blake felt her exhilaration as her mind filled with the knowledge of the gods, but only a fraction of what was possible.

"I know where Odin's eye is hidden," she called, "deep in the wide-famed well of Mimir."

Blake saw that the Eye of Odin would bring what she truly sought, knowledge and power that few could stand against. The monk's broken body fell through the gap in the earth as the seeress stood astride it, head thrown back, shaking as she received the gift of prophecy from the other side of the veil.

***

Blake's visions tunneled and he gasped, his eyes flickering open to find Morgan shaking him.

"Blake, are you OK?" she asked, her eyes concerned and questioning.

"Yes," he whispered. "Just give me a minute."

It took a moment to reorientate himself after reading, like putting on a pair of glasses for the first time and finding the world sharpen in focus to detail never seen before. Every time he read, Blake wondered if this time he would find himself lost somewhere, his mind trapped in another realm, another time, even though his body remained in the modern world. He always set an alarm when he was on his own.

His pulse calmed as he breathed in and out, consciously feeling his physical body on the floor of this room, where he had read so many times.

"There was a Viking raid on a monastery, on an island, a long time ago." He told Morgan of what he had seen, describing the ritual murder of the monk and the words of the seeress in her trance.

"The Eye of Odin," Morgan said, shaking her head. "I've read of this and the story gets stranger indeed. Odin always sought more knowledge, and the legend goes that he visited the Well of Mimir, the Rememberer, in the roots of the world tree, Yggdrasil. The waters revealed the wisdom of the cosmos, and when Odin asked for a drink, Mimir asked for his eye in return. Odin plucked one eye out – which one is unclear – and cast it into the well. In return, Odin drank from the waters. His eye still lies there."

Blake rubbed his temples, the pressure easing him back into his physicality.

"The feeling I got from the seeress was that this Eye is an actual object that can channel prophetic visions from the gods."

Morgan nodded. "The words she spoke have been passed down in the Poetic Edda *Völuspá,* known as the Prophecy of the Seeress. If this Valkyrie wants the Eye too, then the staff can perhaps give her the same visions as the woman you saw."

Blake grimaced. "It seems a sacrifice is needed to activate the staff somehow before the visions come." He described the injuries to the dead monk's body.

"It sounds like the Blood Eagle," Morgan said. "A horrific method of torture and execution where the victim eventually died of blood loss and shock, or through suffocation when the lungs were pulled out through the back. The wings of the splayed ribs represent the eagle, the corpse-gulper, the war-bringer and the bird of Odin."

Blake paled again, knowing that the images would emerge in his nightmares. More bloody bodies to haunt his nights.

"Could you tell where they were?" Morgan asked.

Blake shook his head. "I looked east to the sea as the Vikings ran into the priory. It was certainly an island near the coast, because I could see the land."

"It sounds like Lindisfarne," Morgan said, eyes narrowing as she tried to recall the details. "There were other monastery attacks, but the geographic features sound like the Holy Island. In 793 AD it was the site of the first Viking raid in Britain, a ferocious, surprise attack that left monks dead and much of the treasure from the monastery stolen. They repeated these raids at monasteries on other islands along the Scottish coast, because the sites were so rich."

"There was something else," Blake said, frowning at the memory. "One monk scurried away carrying a heavy book, flanked by several of the others, so it must have been important. Maybe they wrote about the raid in that?"

"The Lindisfarne Gospels are in the British Library," Morgan said. "It's an illuminated manuscript written in the century prior to the invasion. But I seem to remember that there's a page of notes added at the end. It's worth checking out when we get out of here."

An alarm bell rang out suddenly, and both covered their ears to shield them from the high-pitched shriek. When it stopped, an announcement came over the loudspeaker system in the voice of the Valkyrie.

"Bring the staff to the Great Court in the next ten minutes, or I'll start killing hostages."

CHAPTER 6

There was no hesitation in the woman's voice, no room for negotiation, and Morgan knew that their only choice was to go down to the Great Court. She couldn't contact ARKANE – even if she did, a team of agents wouldn't make it here in time to save anyone. She couldn't be sure that the iron staff would even do anything, and besides, once the Valkyrie had it, there was no way for the Neo-Vikings to get out of the museum.

Morgan wished she could go back to this morning, when she had left the ARKANE base under Trafalgar Square ready for a purely civilian research trip. She would have put better procedures in place, brought some kind of weapon with her, and she definitely would have brought backup. Her partner Jake was out on the firing range in the woods of Kent, finally recovered from his injuries, but she should have brought someone else. There was no point in regrets now, though. She could only go forward and take action. Morgan stood.

"We need to go," she said. "I'm not risking lives, and these Neo-Vikings are deadly serious."

Blake stood up, a little unsteady on his feet after the visions. His chiseled features looked pained and his caramel skin was still a shade lighter. Morgan wondered how he coped with the things he saw, how he reconciled it with the physical world of the here and now. She thought back to the demon creature in the bone crypt of Sedlec, how her own worlds had collided then, how her beliefs in what was truly real had been warped and twisted. They had something in common, for sure.

Blake put his gloves back on, covering the ugly scars on his hands. Part of Morgan wanted to touch them, to stroke the lines of years of pain. But if she touched him, could he read her past? Could he see part of her shot to pieces with her husband Elian on the Golan Heights, or blown apart on the streets of Beersheba with her father? She wasn't ready to let anyone come that close.

"We can go through the Mesopotamian Gallery and out by the restaurant," he said, brushing the dust from his jeans. "The stairs lead directly down into the Great Court, but we'll be easily spotted soon enough."

Morgan nodded. "Good, I want them to see us coming. We can't let them harm hostages. Are you OK now?"

Blake rubbed his eyes, blinking. "Yes, sorry. It's a bit of an adjustment coming back." His eyes fell to the staff she held. "Are you sure we should give it to them?"

The staff was cold iron in Morgan's hand, chill metal that only spoke of the dead.

"From what you've said, the real prize is the Eye of Odin, and this staff needs some kind of activation to work its particular magic. Plus, I don't think we have a choice at this stage."

They walked together back through the hall of galleries, emerging through the columns of the classical temple facade that flanked the upper entrance to the Mesopotamian and Egyptian displays. The museum restaurant was empty, nestled in the shadow of the huge round exhibition hall that dominated the central space of the Great Court. White marble steps led down to the ground level entrance. At the top stood one of the Neo-Vikings, his hand on a modern

Glock 26 pistol that looked out of place with his authentic clothing. The man gestured with his gun for them to walk down ahead of him.

Morgan had only been here when the Great Court was packed with tourists, their chatter a hubbub of life in the wide marble space. Now, it was silent except for the sobbing of those below. Their footsteps were loud as they descended the steps, rounding the corner to look down on the forecourt.

"Raise your arms," Morgan whispered as she lifted her own, indicating their surrender, holding the staff high so it could be seen. Blake held his gloved hands up too, his eyes darting to the armed Neo-Vikings that looked up at them.

The hostages were bunched together in a group near the tourist information stand, only a few meters from the front entrance of the museum. Above them, the paneled glass ceiling of the Great Court arched across the space, sun dappling the marble floor with light. Morgan counted five men below with the Valkyrie, and one behind them on the stairs. They were all armed and also held shields now, great metal roundels that made Morgan wonder what they were needed for. She wouldn't expect the British police or military to be storming in here any time soon, not without some negotiation, and even if they did, these shields wouldn't be much use in the face of modern weaponry. But whatever this group had planned, they were surely near the end of it now.

Amongst the faces of the hostages that stared up at them, a few children huddled against their parents. Morgan could see a touch of Gemma in one little girl, and she was thankful that her niece was safe in Oxfordshire. After the sacrifices of Pentecost, she had sworn to make sure her family was never involved in her missions again.

When they reached the bottom of the staircase, two of the Neo-Vikings flanked them as the Valkyrie stepped forward. Morgan held out the staff and the woman took it, her hands mottled with age but her grip as strong as the iron staff itself.

"Why did you take it?" the Valkyrie asked, her eyes piercing.

Morgan stood with shoulders slumped, her head dropped as if she struggled to meet the woman's eyes. "We were scared," she said, her voice humble. "Please … I'm just an academic and I'm doing a paper on the staff. We didn't know you wanted it. We just happened to be there. Truly."

A moment's silence, then the Valkyrie whipped the staff up, smashing it against Blake's cheek. He didn't have time to react, his head snapping sideways. He stumbled and dropped to his knees, clutching his face. A collective gasp came from the hostages.

"No," Morgan cried. Her military instincts kicked in as she moved to take the Valkyrie down, but the big man behind grabbed her, forcing her arm up behind her back in a grip that told Morgan he knew what he was doing. He would not be as easy to defeat as the men upstairs.

"Stay still, or I'll break your arm, bitch," the man whispered.

"It's OK, Morgan. I'm OK. Do what they want, please." Blake was standing again. A cut had opened up high on his cheekbone, and blood began to soak through his gloves as he held his face. Rage bubbled inside Morgan. She longed for a weapon so she could deal with these people, but it wasn't just her life that was at stake here.

"You're clearly not just an academic," the Valkyrie spat. "You sent two of my men back bruised and bloody. They will beat your friend here until you tell the truth, then I'll move on to the children if you continue to lie."

The Neo-Viking pushed Morgan's arm higher, to the edge of breaking it.

"Alright," she said. "I'm Dr. Morgan Sierra, from the Arcane Religious Knowledge And Numinous Experience Institute. I am a researcher, but I'm also ex-Israeli Defense

Force. When the aurora borealis was seen across England and the prophecies about the date of Ragnarok came up in my research, I found a link to this staff. I came to see it for myself."

The Valkyrie nodded. "Then you have seen the days ahead. A storm is coming and you will be a witness for the truth of it, Morgan Sierra. I know of ARKANE. They will be the ones to validate the power of what is to come. And for your truth, I will spare your friend." She turned to her men. "Secure them."

The Neo-Vikings put plastic cuffs on Morgan and Blake, tugging their wrists behind their backs.

"Be a good girl now," the one behind Morgan whispered as he ratcheted the cuffs tight. He licked her ear, his tongue wet and probing. "Or I'll come back and teach you a lesson."

Morgan exhaled deeply, forcing down her natural reaction to turn and teach him a bloody lesson. He would be screaming soon enough, but Blake and the other hostages would pay a price for her anger. She calmed herself.

The men pushed the pair to the floor and put plastic cuffs around their ankles, too. The hostages around them cast surreptitious glances, not wanting to draw attention to themselves. Morgan had seen this reaction before: the urge to keep quiet and avoid the captor's wrath. But she had also seen it in photos, on the faces of those on the train cars, the Jews who had never come home again.

Blake's cheek was swelling, and bruising had already appeared around the cut.

"Are you OK?" Morgan whispered, shuffling closer to him.

He nodded, but she could see he was still reeling from the blow and shocked by the sudden pain. "I'm doing better than him."

Morgan turned to see two of the Neo-Vikings drag the curator out to the front of the hostage group, and push him to kneel in front of the Valkyrie. He stumbled. Morgan could see he was bleeding too, clearly having taken a beating for his insolence in the exhibition hall.

The Valkyrie raised her arms, holding the staff in a tight grip, pointing it to the sky above. It seemed like an extension of her arm and the way she held the heavy metal made it appear lighter … As if it belonged there. In the moment of silence, Morgan heard the faint thrum of a helicopter in the skies above.

"You're witnesses to the beginning of a new age," the Valkyrie said, her voice echoing in the marble hall. "Those of you who are left will report to your media and they will know that Ragnarok is upon us, that I will usher in the final battle by calling up the souls of the dead to vanquish this land like our ancestors did. Too long have we been pathetic in the eyes of the world. Too long have we concerned ourselves with unimportant things. But when the moment of death comes, that is when we realize the triviality of our existence. You will know this soon enough, for a storm is coming."

The helicopter was louder now. Morgan thought perhaps it was the military finally come to free them, or a press helicopter capturing what must be a crazy scene outside.

The Valkyrie began to chant, using the iron staff to spin her words into the air around them. The wind began to blow, lightly at first, as if the doors had been opened to the world outside. It whirled about her as she chanted, the men joining for parts of the incantation, a response to her lead.

"*Nú er blóðugr örn breiðum hjörvi*," she called, her eyes filled with a dread darkness. "Now comes the Blood Eagle with the broadsword."

The curator's head came up, his eyes wild as he clearly understood what she said. He struggled against those who held him.

"No," he screamed. "Not that, please."

He was dragged by two of the men in front of the Valkyrie.

They forced him to his knees and held his mouth open while the seeress poured a dark liquid into his mouth, chanting ancient words of sacrifice. The man slumped into silence within a minute, his eyes glazed over, mouth drooling. The men turned him so his back was to the Valkyrie and ripped his clothes away to reveal his naked torso. The Valkyrie pulled an obsidian knife from her belt, tucking the staff in its place. The light reflected off the surface of the knife. In the glitter, Morgan saw the man's death.

"Great Odin, accept this sacrifice as a herald of the New Age. The Blood Eagle will honor you," the Valkyrie said, her words in English so all could hear. "Hold him tight now."

Two of the men held the curator down as the Valkyrie plunged the knife into his back next to his spine. He screamed despite the sedation and his voice echoed through the Great Court, an animal cry of agony. The Valkyrie began to saw through his ribs and Morgan struggled in her bonds, desperate to stop the atrocity. One of the Viking men backhanded her, making her head ring. She lay stunned on the floor as the Valkyrie carved the curator's body in the ancient way. The hostages around her wept, some frozen with terror, hiding behind each other, desperate not to be next for the slaughter.

As the Valkyrie finished separating a rib she pulled it out and away from the man's body, her hands and arms coated with blood, the men on either side spattered with gore. The curator fell silent and slumped forward, shock shutting down his body, or perhaps dead already from the wounds. But the woman didn't stop. She kept carving and pulling until the ribs formed hideous wings on either side of the man's torso – the wings of the Blood Eagle. Finally, she reached in and pulled the man's lungs from his chest, cutting them from him and offering the chunk of meat to the heavens.

"See this, Odin, and bless our final steps toward glory. Give me your vision now."

The Valkyrie pulled a vial from a pouch at her belt, and sprinkled powder onto the bloody mess of the curator's back. From Blake's description of the Lindisfarne ritual, Morgan thought it must be some kind of powdered relic. The Valkyrie thrust the staff into the wound, coating the iron with fresh blood and powdered bone until it ran red, soaking the sleeves of her tunic.

She held the staff aloft again, spinning around and around, her robes flying out from her. She called out in Norse, a frenzy of blood and power upon her. Her eyes rolled back in her head and she spoke strings of words that Morgan couldn't understand. The Valkyrie was in a shamanic ecstasy, seeing into realms beyond the physical. Could she see where the Eye of Odin lay?

"It is beginning," the Valkyrie called. A vortex of winds seemed to be drawn in, spinning with her, sweeping the dust of the ancient place into the air until it spiraled upwards toward the glass roof. The hostages huddled together, shielding their eyes from the dust that whirled about them, but Morgan needed to see. The Neo-Vikings lifted their shields up over their heads, looking towards the roof as they did so. In that moment, Morgan knew what was going to happen.

CHAPTER 7

THE VALKYRIE THRUST HER staff upward with a shout of triumph. The spiral of wind hit the glass roof with incredible force, smashing the panels, sending a rain of glass down on those below. With a last reserve of energy, Morgan flipped her body and with both feet, sprang for cover as the first shards of glass fell. Blake had the sense to follow her, using his bound feet to push himself along the floor. They made it under the shelter of the tourist information booth before the glass exploded on the marble floor.

Several of the hostages crammed themselves under the overhang along with them, and Morgan pulled one of the children tightly toward her, shielding the little girl's head. Huge shards of glass fractured on the flagstones and the wind whipped the pieces like razors through the crowd as screams echoed through the Great Court. The Valkyrie stood unharmed in the eye of the storm as shards spun around her, while her men were shielded from the large pieces by their shields but were cut by the exploded fragments.

Morgan couldn't take her eyes off the Valkyrie, as she thrust the staff upward again and again. The screams of the captives were peppered with groans as people were cut down while running for cover. It was chaos in the Great Court, but the Neo-Vikings were no longer concerned with the captives.

The vortex smashed against the roof until the metal struts between the glass panes began to warp and bend. A part of Morgan screamed that this must be an illusion – how could the staff hold the power to do this? But the evidence was before her eyes. She could only imagine what it must look like from outside. The sound of smashing glass and howling wind must be heard by the press and police, who were surely now escalating their plans to storm the museum.

When the hole in the roof had stretched across half of the widest part of the Great Court, the Valkyrie stopped her spinning. The wind died down. The sound of a helicopter grew louder, and then it appeared, a shadow against the blue sky above. It was a Black Hawk, the open door revealing two men inside as well as the pilot. Hovering directly above, they lowered a winch basket that descended to the floor of the museum. The Valkyrie didn't even look back at the hostages. She entered the basket and two of the Neo-Vikings entered with her, all three holding tight to the mesh sides.

They can't possibly get away, Morgan thought. A helicopter this low over London would have the military out after them. They weren't so far from Parliament and Buckingham Palace, after all. Concern flashed through her mind, for this group was clearly well funded. This was not the work of a two-bit cult in furs. Everything in Morgan wished for a weapon to stop them, to punish them for what they had done. Instead, she lay with Blake under the overhang, unable to do anything to stop the escape.

"Your sacrifice has earned you a place in Valhalla," the Valkyrie said to the men who would be left behind. Two nodded, watching as the basket was winched up to the helicopter above the museum.

"No, take me too," one of the men shouted, his eyes wide with fear of what would befall him if left behind. He ran wildly for the cage, which was now just six feet from the ground. The man jumped and caught hold of the bottom, his fingers protruding into the cage. The winch shuddered and inched up more slowly.

"Let go," the men in the basket shouted, stamping at his fingers. "It's too heavy."

The cage inched higher and the man still held on.

"Please," he screamed. "Don't leave me."

As the cage reached the upper third of the open space, the Valkyrie bent and slashed at the man's fingers with her knife. When he still didn't let go, she began to saw at them.

"No," he screamed as blood ran down his arm. Finally, he couldn't hold on anymore. He let go, his scream silenced as he smashed into the flagstones, his blood running into the words of Tennyson carved in the marble floor of the Great Court.

The cage was winched up the final meters and the Valkyrie and her men pulled into the helicopter as it banked away out of sight, the noise of the blades fading as it flew off. Morgan's resolve was steel, refined by the heat of her rage at the murder of the curator, the injuries to the hostages and the despoiling of this great museum. She would hunt down this Valkyrie and get the staff back, and she would find the Eye of Odin.

The Neo-Vikings left behind threw their shields down. Without looking at the hostages, they ran toward the back of the museum. The hostages, many cut and bleeding, sat in stunned silence for a moment. Then one man stood up and walked toward the entrance, his steps halting as if he couldn't believe he was free to go.

There was a crash from the museum's front entrance and a team of armed police and medics swarmed in, one wrapping the man in a blanket as they passed to triage those huddled on the marble floor. A policeman called for body bags and soon the hall was alive with activity, processing the crime scene and helping those with injuries to waiting ambulances. Several of the armed police headed toward the back of the building, but Morgan considered that this was so well planned, the Neo-Vikings may well have got away unseen.

In the group of medics that entered, Morgan saw Peter Lovell, one of the ARKANE London support team. With fifteen years as a military doctor, Peter's buzz cut, upright posture and confident bearing made him stand out, and he was definitely overqualified for this type of first aid care. He came straight to her, ignoring all the others, leaving them to the official emergency services.

"Morgan, are you OK?" Peter asked. "Where are you hurt?"

"Just get these cuffs off," she said, holding her wrists out as he reached into his bag for a scalpel. "This is Blake." Morgan nodded to the side, where Blake sat staring up at the hole in the magnificent glass roof. "He has a head wound that needs to be dealt with before you look at me properly."

"Director Marietti wants you back at base ASAP, if you're OK," Peter said. "I'll take you back now and leave this lot to the crime scene techs. ARKANE will help the police coordinate the search with expert help on where the Neo-Vikings might have gone."

"Let me guess," Morgan's mouth twisted in a wry smile as he finished cutting her cuffs. "I'm the expert help."

Once Morgan's wrists were free, Peter cut away the restraints on her feet and then did the same for Blake.

"I'm going to find them," Morgan said, her hand resting on Blake's upper arm, feeling the tension under his skin. "I'll get the staff back and they'll pay for what they did to the curator."

Blake looked over to where the body of the mutilated man was being lifted onto a stretcher.

"He was a cantankerous old bastard sometimes, but he was a respected colleague and pretty fun at Christmas parties."

He smiled painfully at the memory and turned to Morgan, his blue eyes meeting hers, and she saw that his resolve matched hers.

"I want to help. You know what I can do, and if we want to find them quickly, I think we need to check out The Lindisfarne Gospels. They might have a clue as to what happened to the original Valkyrie." He turned his head so Peter could clean his wound, wincing with the sting of the antiseptic on his bruised skin and open cut.

Morgan knew that Director Marietti wouldn't like involving a civilian, but the London ARKANE office didn't have anyone with psychometric ability – not that she knew of, anyway.

Her only hesitation was that she had a bad habit of involving other people who ended up getting hurt. Morgan thought of Dr. Khal el-Souid, badly beaten in the caves of Mount Nebo as they searched for the Ark of the Covenant. He'd been lucky to escape with only minor concussion. She blushed a little as she remembered the night that followed. Khal's dark eyes meeting hers in the light of the early morning as the muezzin called the dawn prayers … How his arms had felt around her. She and Khal had shared something in the desert, but Morgan knew a relationship was never going to work, so she had left him behind and they hadn't spoken since. Blake reminded her a little of Khal, a smart man with gorgeous skin, his blue eyes the ocean to Khal's deep brown. She pushed aside her concerns. Blake was involved now, whether she liked it or not, and she needed his help for just a little longer.

"I'm sorry, Peter. I'll call Marietti en route, but we need to go to the British Library before I head back."

CHAPTER 8

Morgan and Blake jumped in a black cab and headed for the British Library, only a few blocks northeast toward St Pancras station. Morgan finally had reception to make a call and dialed Director Marietti's personal phone.

"Morgan, are you all right?" The gruff voice of the Director was tempered by concern. "I'm viewing some of the security camera footage now, and it's brutal stuff."

"Yes, I'm fine sir, and I'll report in full soon, but right now we have a lead that may help us locate where the Neo-Viking group are heading. Were the police able to track the helicopter?"

"The Neo-Vikings used the same type of Black Hawk helicopter as the Americans allegedly used for the raid on Bin Laden. It doesn't show up on radar, but we're tracking physical sightings right now. They flew east, then must have landed either on a boat or transferred to land transport."

Morgan frowned. "It suggests some serious funding behind the group."

"Exactly." Marietti's voice held the promise of further investigation. "There was also a vicious wind that surrounded the helicopter as they headed east, low over the river toward the sea. Nothing could get close to it. I want you back here to work on what the hell is going on."

"The leader of the group was a woman calling herself the Valkyrie, and she said some things that reminded one of the academics at the museum of The Lindisfarne Gospels." Morgan didn't want to try and explain Blake's unique ability right now, especially as she knew that Marietti might try to recruit him or at least want to know a lot more than she had time for. "The researcher is with me now, and we're going to check the Gospels out. Can you call ahead and get that cleared so we have access?"

Morgan heard the hesitation in Marietti's voice.

"All right, go check the Gospels, but then you've got to get back here, Morgan. The press are having a field day with this. While the police work on the crime angle, we need to get that staff back. Based on the footage of the Valkyrie and the wind she generated, there are plenty of people who are going to want it."

Morgan knew that there was an underground network of organizations and individuals who collected such objects. Most of them kept to the shadows, but others emerged with their plans to impact the wider world. The staff of Skara Brae, resonating with ancient power, would draw them all when the footage was inevitably released on YouTube. Some would dismiss it as fake special effects, the conspiracy theorists would turn it into the start of some global plot, but some would know the truth and seek it out. The staff was powerful in the right hands, and Morgan knew she had to get it back. If they could locate the Eye of Odin as well, then all the better.

***

The taxi pulled up in front of the British Library on the Euston Road. Morgan and Blake walked into the forecourt, past the huge bronze statue of Newton, bent to measure the world with his calipers, frowning with concentration. The British Library was a modern building, red brick on two sides of the piazza square, with the gothic spires of St Pancras station towering behind it. Three flagpoles stood in the middle of the square, the Union Jack fluttering in the breeze, while readers streamed in the doors or drank coffee in patches of sun, fingers flicking through books. Despite the modern exterior, this library was a treasure store of the written word, a nirvana for any bibliophile. Morgan loved to come here, to feel a part of the grand heritage that was England.

"I'm not sure we can just walk in and demand to see The Lindisfarne Gospels," Blake said, as they walked across the square.

"We won't have to," Morgan said. "ARKANE has phoned ahead."

Blake chuckled. "I envy you. My research is usually a combination of my own psychometric reading and then a period of begging for access to get it verified through official sources."

The entrance to the library was flanked by security guards who nodded them through, and they stepped into the spacious atrium. Sun streamed down from skylights high above the central light well, and three levels of reading rooms could be seen, with readers bustling between them carrying the clear plastic bags that were mandatory in the Reading Rooms. The sense was of open space, not crammed stacks, a portal to the information housed here in so many forms, much of it now digitized.

"The Gospels are in the Ritblat Gallery, alongside the other Treasures of the Library," Morgan said. "This way."

Up a short flight of stairs, the entrance to the Ritblat Gallery was dark, the light dimmed to preserve the precious objects within. Each glass case held priceless documents, from pages of Leonardo da Vinci's notebooks to an eleventh-century manuscript of *Beowulf*, the handwritten pages damaged by fire. Thomas Hardy's original manuscript of *Tess of the D'Urbervilles* was here, his fine cross-hatched edits still evident, as well as more modern treasures like the lyrics to The Beatles' "Yesterday."

A huge globe dominated one area of the room, a baroque vision of the heavens painted with ancient constellation figures. Pegasus, the winged horse, galloped next to the Great Bear, paws uplifted to stride across the globe. Nearby stood the collection of Christian manuscripts, most illuminated by the hands of monks long dead.

Morgan couldn't help but look into the case holding the Codex Sinaiticus, her thoughts going back to St Catherine's Monastery in the Sinai, where it had originally been kept. Written over 1600 years ago, the handwritten manuscript with heavily corrected text was the Christian Bible in Greek, containing the oldest complete copy of the New Testament. Pages of the text had been sewn into other book bindings, and a fragment had pointed her and Khal to a new location for the Ark of the Covenant not so long ago. Despite the dangers of ARKANE, Morgan lived on the edge of the boundary between the ancient world and the modern, and there was nowhere else she would rather work.

A librarian waved at them from a side door.

"Are you from ARKANE?" the woman asked. Morgan nodded. "The Lindisfarne Gospels are normally kept on display here, but they're currently resting."

"Resting?" Blake asked.

The librarian gave him a smile as she touched her hair, her eyes twinkling more as she addressed him directly. Blake's injuries only seemed to heighten his good looks.

"Even though the lights are dimmed in here, the manuscripts are still affected so we like to give them a rest in the dark now and then. Our aim at the British Library is to make sure these treasures last another thousand years for everyone to enjoy. Normally we wouldn't allow anything to disturb them, but you seem to have a special pass. We've just retrieved the Gospels from their resting place and they're ready for you to view. Follow me."

The woman pushed open a door leading away from the Ritblat Gallery, and walked ahead of them down a short corridor. At a doorway, she turned, pulling two pairs of white gloves wrapped in plastic from her pocket.

"These are mandatory for you to wear when handling the manuscript." She frowned, noticing Blake's own gloves for the first time. He turned his hands so she couldn't see the blood stains.

"Of course," Morgan said, taking them and handing a pair to Blake.

They pulled off the plastic and put the gloves on, Blake hiding his own stained pair in his pocket for the meantime. When she was satisfied they were appropriately attired, the librarian pushed open the door.

"I've been told to leave you to it, but I'll just be down the hall if you need anything."

Morgan and Blake stepped into the room, a stark white cube containing nothing but a white table with a bookrest, and on it, The Lindisfarne Gospels. The book was illuminated with artistic calligraphy and painted scenes, interweaving the cultures that influenced England at the time it was written. There were Egyptian Coptic cross-carpet pages, exotic iconography from the Eastern Mediterranean, Celtic spiral patterns, Greek Byzantine lettering and even the angular shapes of Germanic runes. Created in the late seventh century at Lindisfarne Priory, the book was considered to be one of the nation's leading artistic treasures, as well as an icon of faith.

"It's beautiful," Blake said, bending to look at the cover more closely. Gold and silver strips formed a border around the edge, each with a precious stone in the middle. The center panel was a deep crimson inlaid with Celtic woven patterns in precious metal, a fitting cover for such a holy book.

Morgan opened the first page with gloved fingers, revealing a richly colored tapestry of red and sunset-yellow tiles around the shape of a cross. The Coptic carpet style was reminiscent of Islamic prayer rugs, and miniature birds lay around the edge, beaks clutching each other's feet in a never-ending spiral. The letters at the beginning of the Gospels were illuminated in the colors of turquoise, ochre and plum, each one a world of fantastical beasts and swirling heraldic devices.

"It looks like there is other writing under the main text," Blake said.

"It's a translation," Morgan pointed, careful not to touch the page. "Old English was added between the lines of Latin, which makes it one of the oldest surviving translations of the Gospels into English. I wish we had time to study it properly, but we should really just check the back page. A colophon was added after the Viking invasion."

She slowly turned the pages, glimpsing paintings of the gospel writers transcribing the words of the Lord while angels trumpeted behind them, until finally, the last page was revealed. After the glorious extravagance and riot of color throughout the book, the colophon was an anticlimax, a page of black text, with the translation underneath and a column of text in a more casual hand, almost running off the edge of the page.

"It's a list of who helped in the making of the Gospels, but there's some text that scholars have struggled to translate." She pointed. "Right here. It's only a few lines."

"Perhaps if I try my kind of reading, I'll be able to get a sense of what the scribe was getting at." Blake pulled one of the white gloves off. "Although to be honest, I've not had much luck reading manuscripts, as they usually have so many people involved in making them."

"This one is different," Morgan said. "It's supposed to be the work of one man, attributed to Bishop Eadfrith of Lindisfarne."

"We might have a chance then. Keep an eye on the door, will you? I don't want to suffer the wrath of the librarian if I'm caught touching this book. I've had quite enough violence for one day."

Blake laid his bare fingers lightly on the edge of the handwritten text and closed his eyes.

CHAPTER 9

THE CRY OF SEAGULLS pierced the veil of Blake's consciousness and the smell of the sea made him long for ocean winds. He opened his eyes to see the ruins of Lindisfarne Priory. Cottages still burned and the remains of slaughtered animals and men lay in the streets, in the direct aftermath of the Viking attack. Blake felt the outrage of the monk who held the Gospels tightly to his breast, and the grief that washed over his soul at what must surely be the loss of what he called family.

"Come, brother." The words were rough and cut with emotion. "We can do no more here. We must get word to Eilean Idhe, for that witch and her pagan protectors were searching for something and I'm afraid what they seek has been long hidden there. If we hurry, we can make the tidal crossing and begin our long journey before the waters get too high."

Blake turned to see another monk by his side, pulling the cowl up over his tonsured head to keep the wind from his weathered face, or perhaps to hide his tears. The land had been etched in his visage and his eyes were a deep brown, like the earth beneath their feet. He strode off, and Blake lengthened his stride to keep up, feeling a strange sense of the physical body he inhabited albeit briefly. The man who clutched the Gospels to his chest was muscular yet wiry, with strength in his limbs and a clarity of purpose that made every step a statement of survival despite persecution.

As dusk began to fall, they emerged at a headland and Blake saw the crossing. A narrow strip of land ran from the island to the shore while the ocean lapped on either side, each minute reclaiming the wet ground for the sea. Lindisfarne was cut off from the mainland for all but a short time every day, a separate community of those who served God. Blake felt a sense of trepidation well up within him as he looked at the thin sliver of land left. They would be wading soon, and the waters would continue to rise, the current strong against their legs. Could he dare take the precious package of the Gospels from this place?

The other monk turned.

"We must hurry, brother. Come quickly, or the waters will be too high." He reached out his hand. "I will help you."

At his kind words, Blake felt the monk relax and his faith in God calming him. The terrors of the day faded as the two men walked into the rising waters and Blake's grip on the moment began to fade, the intense emotions around the book dissipating.

He sifted through layers of consciousness, searching for another strand to grab onto, desperate to find out where the monks were heading and learn of the mysterious reference to what was hidden at this other place. In the layers between time, he found a glimmer of revelation and pulled himself back into the monk's awareness.

***

The two monks stepped off a little boat onto a beach of pale sand. Blake could sense their exhaustion after a long and dangerous journey. He had his back to a stretch of water, and the sun was setting directly ahead behind verdant green hills. A small village of low huts with a wooden church at its center loomed ahead in silhouette.

The monk, still carrying the Gospels, fell to his knees.

"Blessed St Columba, we thank you for your protection on this journey." His prayers were fervent, cut short as a welcoming shout came from the monastery and brothers came to meet them.

***

Blake was jolted out of the trance as Morgan removed his hand from the book.

"Quick," she said. "Put the glove back on. Someone's coming."

Blake pulled the white glove on, his head reeling from the shift in perspective. How strange to be on an island one moment and then here in this surgically clean space in central London. Vertigo made his head spin and he clutched the edge of the table as the door opened.

"Are you all right in here?" the librarian asked, her eyes narrowing as she saw Blake sagging a little. He stood up straighter, giving her his best rakish smile, an implied invitation that made her blush and avert her eyes quickly.

"Yes, of course," Morgan said. "We just need a few more minutes."

"Sure," the librarian said, giving Blake a smile before she left again, the door closing behind her.

"What did you do to her?" Morgan asked, grinning at Blake. "I might invite you to be my sidekick again if you charm all the ladies that way."

Blake thought of the nights he spent under the wicked spell of tequila, the casual sexual conquests on the London nightlife scene, the practice that lay under his easy sexuality.

Where once those ephemeral pleasures had satisfied him, he now began to sense the emptiness in his life choices, but Morgan didn't need to know about that side of his life.

"Just my inimitable charm," he said. "Before you pulled me back, I did discover a couple of things that might help us. The Gospels were carried away from Lindisfarne by two monks, heading for another place where the sun set behind the hills and a strip of ocean was to my back, the reverse of Lindisfarne."

"Another island, but on the west coast, you think?"

Blake nodded. "Yes, and they said something about needing to warn a community about the raids, that the thing the Vikings sought was buried there … they called it Eilean Idhe, but I'm sure I'm massacring the pronunciation."

Morgan smiled, recognition dawning on her face.

"The island is called Iona now. It's still a spiritual community, rich in the Christian tradition. The Bishop of Lindisfarne, St Cuthbert, originally came from Iona, so it makes sense there were ties between the two. The Vikings also raided the island in 794 and for many years afterwards, so perhaps they never found what they sought that day. Perhaps the monks warned them in time."

Blake heard the curiosity in her voice. "You're going there, aren't you?"

Morgan nodded. "If you think that's where the Valkyrie is heading, then yes, I'll go … but with some backup this time."

Blake knew this was probably the end of his time with Morgan, but his experiences with Jamie Brooke on the Hunterian murder and now this were helping him to see that his gift could be useful. Perhaps there could be a way to use it to help, rather than just to see visions that haunted his nightmares.

"Need a sidekick?" Blake asked, turning on his most charming smile. Morgan laughed, and he chuckled along with her, for there was no entrancing this woman. She was smart as well as attractive and saw right through his attempts. Morgan put her hand on his arm, suddenly serious.

"Thank you for your help with this, Blake. Now I can use this information to go after the Valkyrie."

"Will I ... see you again?" he asked, not wanting this to be the end. "I want to know what you find, and I doubt that I'll find any kind of truth in the media. At least our kind of truth anyway."

Morgan hesitated, then nodded. "I'll find you afterwards, I promise. Why don't you stay and look at the Gospels for a bit longer. I'm sure the librarian would be happy to take you on a personal tour."

As they both laughed, Morgan leaned forward and kissed Blake on the cheek. He looked into her blue eyes, like cobalt from the illuminated script, the slash of violet in her right darker now, almost indigo. He wanted to read her, wanted to know her emotions, and her past. She intrigued him.

"This is goodbye for now," she said, turning to the door and walking out, without looking back.

***

Morgan pulled out her phone in the atrium of the library. Marietti answered on the first ring.

"Did you find anything?" he asked, his voice tense. She could hear talking in the background, and a news bulletin that still looped on the museum hostage crisis.

"I think they might be heading to Iona," Morgan said. "The Scottish island also had a famous monastery that was raided by the Vikings, and it could be that they were looking for the same thing the Valkyrie is. She called it the Eye of Odin, and the staff was just a step on that journey. The museum wasn't the end game."

"Hmm. Interesting, but things look a little different from here. We've had a report of a suspicious murder in the Orkney Islands, a man ritually killed in the Ring of Brodgar, a Neolithic stone circle. The local police say there's a group who follow the ways of the Vikings in the islands, expected back later tonight. Harmless, or so they thought." Marietti laughed bitterly. "I'm sending a team there to investigate and intercept the return of the Valkyrie."

It was over 200 miles from Orkney to Iona across land and sea, Morgan thought. If she was wrong, then she would miss out on dispensing the justice she so desperately wanted. Betting on Blake's visions over hard evidence was crazy, but she thought of how he had been in the trance. It was as if he had left his physical body, and working for ARKANE had eroded the skepticism she used to have about the inexplicable.

"I'd like to go to Iona," she said. "Then we'll be covering both angles."

"Hold on a minute." Morgan heard Marietti barking commands to those in his office before returning to the phone. "Alright, get to Iona. But if you insist on investigating there, I can't spare anyone to come with you. We're stretched as it is, and you might find nothing. We can send backup if you do get a lead. Still want to go?"

Morgan's rage about the murder in the museum was still simmering, and she didn't want to continue this fight back in the depths of the ARKANE offices. Her preference was always for action, if she had the choice. Of course, Blake's unusual talent could be completely useless, his visions merely the product of an unhinged mind. But she had seen him read, and there had been no trace of the crazy there, only a man who was tortured by what he saw.

"Yes, I want to go. But can you at least get me a weapon?"

"Head for London City Airport and we'll sort out a flight to Glasgow, and a helicopter from there. There'll be a box waiting for you. Stay in touch, Morgan."

Marietti hung up and Morgan stood in the busy atrium of the library, surrounded by the bustle of the readers, wondering whether this was the right decision. She appreciated Marietti's trust, his lack of micromanagement of his team, but she also felt a little alone without her partner, or without even Blake at her side. Then, she remembered the grotesque death of the curator, the violence of the Valkyrie in her quest. She pushed open the doors and headed for the taxi rank.

CHAPTER 10

Morgan stepped off the charter boat onto the white sandy shores of Iona, turning back to take her bag from the charter boat skipper. One of the Inner Hebrides, Iona was situated off the southwest tip of the Isle of Mull. West from the island was the broad Atlantic, all the way to Newfoundland. The charter flight to Glasgow, the helicopter to Mull, and finally the boat to Iona had only taken a couple of hours, but this place was another world compared to the teeming city she'd left behind.

The light was beginning to fade as Morgan looked around at the little village of Baile Mòr, its stone houses staring back toward the mainland. This was a hardy land, with a small population who preferred isolation and solitude to the bustle of the city. Morgan could only imagine the hell London would be for these people, for here time was measured by the tides, the shifting wind and the cry of the skylark.

A little way from the village streets, the mottled stone walls of the Iona Abbey stood proud, built on the site of the monastery founded by St Columba in the mid-sixth century. It had been a beacon for early Christianity, influencing the spread of faith amongst the Picts and the Scots. Although she had been brought up in Israel, her father Jewish, Morgan felt a momentary longing to find a bed in one of the Christian retreat centers and just close her eyes. The intensity of her missions with ARKANE had taken their toll, and she had the sense that things were only speeding up, that the world was spiraling toward some kind of terrifying end. The glimpses she had experienced were only one piece of the information, but she knew that Marietti understood some of the bigger picture. The ARKANE director had become haggard of late, his beard whitening in recent months. Perhaps it was almost time to ask him to share what he knew.

"Can I help you, lassie?" The broad Scottish accent was welcoming. "I saw you coming from the boat there." The man wore just a t-shirt despite the chilling wind, his bare arms roped with muscle as he carried a box wrapped in brown paper toward the charter boat that was preparing to leave again. His face was rugged, with deep laughter lines. "Are you with those others?"

It had to be the Valkyrie's group, Morgan thought. They had a head start on her, but they couldn't have been here too long.

"Yes, I'm with them," she smiled as she spoke, "but I missed a connection. Do you know where they went?"

"They're up at the abbey, all dressed up it seems. But we get all sorts here, to be sure."

The man shook his head. So many pilgrims came here to worship and pay homage to history, to find their sense of God in this wide open space, that Morgan guessed he witnessed a lot of strange people coming through.

"Thank you for your help."

The man walked toward the boat, calling to the others to wait up for his package. Morgan bent to her small pack, and with her body shielding the view from the boat, she checked to ensure the Barak SP-21 pistol was loaded.

A rumble of thunder made her lift her head to the sky. Toward the west, dark clouds were gathering and the wind was picking up. Fat drops of rain began to splatter down and a chill pierced the air. Morgan thought of the vortex the Valkyrie had commanded back at the museum, and looked up towards the Benedictine abbey. The light was dim now, but she could just make out figures in front of the twelfth-century stone building.

Morgan pulled her hood up and tugged the thick coat closer around her as she walked quickly up the main street toward the abbey. It was known as the *Reilig Odhráin*, Road of the Dead, where the funeral procession would walk with the body of Christian dead to be buried in the abbey grounds. Early Kings of Scotland were buried here, including *Mac Bethad mac Findlaích*, known to history as Macbeth.

The darkness grew thicker now as clouds billowed above in shades of violet, shot through with flickering lightning. The few people remaining outside in the streets ran for cover, closing windows and preparing for the storm. They were used to the vagaries of the weather on this peninsula by the Atlantic, with nothing to shield them from the elements. Now, Morgan was counting on it to disguise her approach to the abbey as she crept to the edge of the great medieval building.

As she drew closer, Morgan saw the Valkyrie standing in the rain, a fur wrap covering her gray tunic, her hair plastered to her head as the drops ran unheeded down her face. There was steel in the old woman's posture, a hardness in her features and a new knowledge that darkened her eyes. She held the staff of Skara Brae in front of her, gnarled fingers clutching it tightly.

Three of the Neo-Vikings were digging under the base of the eighth-century St Martin's Cross. The ring behind the medieval cross symbolized eternity and the presence of a halo, and the stone was carved with scenes from the Bible. Even from a short distance away, Morgan recognized Daniel in the lion's den, Abraham with sword raised to sacrifice Isaac, and writhing serpents around circular bosses. One of the men pushed against the heavy stone, rocking his body back and forth to try to move it.

"No," a voice cried. A man ran out from the cover of the abbey doorway, clearly one of the clergy. "That cross has stood by the grace of God for over 1200 years on that spot. You can't just knock it down."

He grabbed the arm of the Neo-Viking, who laughed, a deep rumbling sound, and reached around the back of the man's head, yanking it forward to smash against the stone. The clergyman groaned in pain and slumped a little, but the Neo-Viking pulled him forward again, driving his skull onto the arm of the cross, blood now oozing from the wound, staining the ancient stone.

"Enough," the Valkyrie said, her Scottish lilt a direct order. "Finish digging. The Eye is under there, I've seen it in my visions. It calls to the staff now. Dig harder."

The Neo-Viking threw the clergyman to the ground, where he lay clutching his head as the rain slammed down upon his prone body. Morgan willed him to stay still and just wait. Even with a weapon, she couldn't stop all of them, and with people in the abbey, she didn't want to risk making a move. She pulled back around the edge of the building and texted Marietti at ARKANE, informing him that the group was there, though she knew that backup wouldn't get here in time to stop the Neo-Vikings recovering the Eye of Odin. If she was honest, part of Morgan wanted to see what happened when the Eye was recovered. She was drawn to the edge of darkness, for the glimpses she had seen into the realm of miracle had given her a taste of something beyond the mundane world.

A loud rumble of thunder echoed across the bay, followed quickly by a crack of lightning. The storm was almost upon them. Morgan peered around again to see the Neo-Vikings pushing the stone cross to the ground, its granite pedestal split open. The Valkyrie knelt before it, her hands thrust into the earth. She pulled out a slim metal box and held it to the sky, rain hammering down upon her uplifted arms.

"For you, Odin. *Skelfr Yggdrasils askr standandi, ymr it aldna tré, en jötunn losnar,*" she called to the heavens. "Yggdrasil shakes, shiver on high the ancient limbs, and the giant is loose."

The triumph in her voice sent a shiver down Morgan's spine. The words the Valkyrie spoke were from the *Völuspá*, a prophecy of the end times, heralding the battle known to the Vikings as Ragnarok.

The Valkyrie opened the box and her men gathered close behind her to look inside. The expression on their faces was one of wonder, and more than that, of visceral desire. Morgan had seen that look before, on the faces of those who saw the huge gems of the Jewel House in the Tower of London and coveted them. The Valkyrie lifted the object from the box and turned to the men, the lump of yellow rock in her hands. There was a fire inside the precious stone, a burning that turned its facets to gold even in the darkened world around. The raindrops seemed to bring it alive. Odin's Eye was said to shine like the sun, and this rock looked to be a huge piece of rare yellow diamond, worth many millions. Morgan knew it would serve a darker purpose tonight.

"We must go to the west for the summoning," the Valkyrie said, looking up into the swirling clouds, eyes unblinking in the heavy rain. She indicated the injured man on the ground. "Bring him."

CHAPTER 11

Morgan stepped back quietly to hide in the shadow of the abbey as the Valkyrie and her men passed close by, dragging the moaning clergyman between them. The group entered a car and drove away into the rainy night. Morgan had checked the maps and seen the famous Bay at the Back of the Ocean, a wide west-facing sweep of white sand looking out across the sea to North America. It was just over the other side of the island, but too far to walk or run. She looked around the car park, spotting a mountain bike alongside a low fence. It wasn't locked, as these islands hadn't been a crime hotspot. Until tonight.

Grabbing the bike, Morgan pedaled hard after the car toward the west of the island. The rain lashed down upon her, but she soon warmed as her breath came hard, heart beating fast with the exertion and apprehension of what was to come. Could the Valkyrie really summon the final destiny of the gods with the Eye of Odin?

As she pedaled faster, rising to her feet to push hard up the hill, Morgan smiled, an almost manic excitement rising within her. In one sense, she had never felt so alone, with no backup, her partner Jake at the other end of the country, her family not even knowing what she was doing or where she was. But she also recognized that the thrill of the edge was what she constantly sought. It made her feel alive. If she should die here today, it would be with the grin of the berserker on her face, going to meet her fate laughing at the gods.

At the crest of the hill, Morgan paused to catch her breath and, through the rain, saw the headlights of the car near the rocky headland. A mist was rising from the earth: the smell of wild thyme and the salty tang of the ocean spray hung fresh in the air. The sound of the waves on the beach could be heard beneath the thump of the rain, and the crackle of lightning burst through the charged air, the forked silver striking the rocks below.

She let the bike freewheel down the hill and then left it so she could continue on foot, creeping through the rocks at the edge of the bay, hiding behind one to peer through at the tableau.

One of the Neo-Vikings pushed the clergyman to his knees on the rocks as the Valkyrie began to spin the staff, holding the Eye of Odin in her other hand. A shrill cawing filled the air. Morgan looked up to see a flock of dark birds, the ravens of the island, begin to fly in a circle in an eerie reflection of the movements below. The Valkyrie whirled the staff, weaving patterns in the air, chanting in a voice that grated against something in Morgan's very soul.

"*Snýsk jörmungandr í jötunmóði,*" the Valkyrie called into the spinning vortex that materialized around her. "In giant-wrath does the serpent writhe."

With those words, she pointed the staff at the kneeling clergyman. The Neo-Viking behind him pulled the man's head back and sliced his throat with a heavy knife. Arterial blood sprayed into the whirling tornado around the Valkyrie, the droplets whipped into the spiraling air until it was as if she stood within a wall of blood that the rain could no longer penetrate. The Eye of Odin glowed in her hand, its light illuminating her face, a prophet of long-dead gods.

The Valkyrie turned to face the vast expanse of the Atlantic.

"*Ormr knýr unnir, en ari hlakkar, slítr nái niðfölr.*" Her voice was a shriek now, rising above the rumble of thunder that echoed around the bay. "Over the waves he twists, and the tawny eagle gnaws corpses screaming."

She stretched out the staff and held the Eye of Odin close to it. Through the veil of blood, the golden light from the stone looked like a ray of the sun as it shot out into the boiling sea below. It seemed to carve a path in the water, some kind of bioluminescence revealing the depths below.

One of the Neo-Vikings lifted a great curved horn to his lips and blew it, the deep sound a sonorous vibration that shook the rocks they stood upon. The other two Neo-Vikings dropped to their knees, as the waters boiled and in the distance, Morgan thought she saw coils of some great creature arching from the deep. The legends of Ragnarok told of *Jörmungandr*, the Midgard serpent that encircles the earth holding his tail in his mouth until the day he lets go and the world ends.

Morgan tried to focus on what she thought she had seen, but between flashes of lightning, it could have been nothing more than waves. The Neo-Vikings were transfixed by the sight of the golden ray, and she knew she needed to finish this. She pulled the gun from her pack. The power of this staff, the Eye of Odin ... It all needed to end here.

The Valkyrie stood with arms pointed toward the deep, the wall of spinning blood around her, and it seemed to Morgan that she began to lift from the rock to hang in the air. The ravens flew faster around the top of the vortex, a dark host crowing the victory of those who worshipped the ancient gods, calling for their return.

Aiming for the Valkyrie's back, Morgan fired once, twice, but the bullets ricocheted off the vortex, one hitting a Neo-Viking in the eye on rebound. He slumped to the ground without a sound, but the other two men jumped to their feet, roaring with anger. The Valkyrie turned her head at the noise and her hands faltered, the light from the staff and the Eye wobbling in the water. She refocused, chanting louder with darker words, her eyes rolling back in her head as she floated upward. The boiling in the ocean seemed to double in intensity and lightning strikes hit the waters with a hiss, the clouds above whirling in a tornado. Something was coming, something from the other side.

Morgan left her hiding place, leaping across the rocks sideways to the Valkyrie. One of the men moved to shield his mistress and the other pursued. Morgan turned and shot again. A double tap and the man went down, his bulk falling between the rocks.

Only one man stood between her and the witch now. Holding the gun out, Morgan stepped across the rocks, hyper-alert as the man held his arms wide, inviting her to him. She aimed at his mid-section, finger squeezing the trigger. The moment she fired, a sharp tug on her ankle pulled her down and pain exploded as Morgan's knee cracked on the sharp rocks. The man she had shot first reached up to grab her, his face a mess of blood where his head had hit the rocks, the chest wound bleeding but not fatal. Losing her grip, the gun went clattering down the side of the rocks.

Morgan kicked backward, ignoring the pain as she smashed her boot into the man's face. Her Krav Maga military training took over, and she put every ounce of force into her kick. The man's head flicked back, and he lost his grip on her ankle. Morgan turned, using her momentum to push herself up from the rocks and kicked at the man's head, connecting with his temple with a sickening crunch. Breathing hard now, Morgan's vision narrowed. Her senses heightened, she heard the sound of the ocean boiling, the crows cawing, the Valkyrie chanting, and felt an electricity in the air as the veil of reality shifted.

Aware of danger from behind, she turned to see the other Neo-Viking almost upon her, his eyes wild. The gun was out of reach now and Morgan bent her knees, her palms outstretched in the waiting Krav Maga stance. The man lumbered toward her, over six feet of muscle, his face tattooed with Norse runes, a mark of devotion to his gods. He grimaced. Morgan saw his teeth were filed and marked with black.

"I will rip your throat out," he taunted, "and the Valkyrie will feed your corpse to great *Jörmungandr.*"

He ran at her, leaping over the rocks, hands outstretched. Morgan waited for him to get close, willing him to attack so she could hurt him. The blood lust was high within her now. She wanted to beat this man into the earth and leave his bones to rot.

The man led with a punch. Morgan brushed his hand aside with an open palm, using the other arm to slam her elbow into his temple as she shouted her rage, her voice coming from a primal place of survival. She followed through with hammerfist strikes that made the man reel. But he kept coming, head lower now, swaying a little. Morgan didn't relent. She went toward him again and as he tried to grab her waist to pull her to the floor, she grabbed his ears, twisting them with a savage yell. She used all her strength to spring from the rocks with one knee lifted and slammed it into his face, once, twice, as fast as the lightning strikes above. The man went down and Morgan leaned in, using her bent knuckles to slam into his throat.

Leaving the man gurgling for breath, Morgan turned back to the Valkyrie. Either side of the golden ray of light, the ocean was forming a wall of white water and violent waves, a path for whatever was summoned. Morgan felt the world hum in the pulsing throb of the golden light, the pounding of the waves and the triumphant chant of the Valkyrie, her thin body transformed into power.

The gun was useless now, but there was still a chance to disrupt whatever was coming. Morgan ran at the vortex, pushing off the rocks to leap through the wall of blood, her rage exploding in a primordial roar. She slammed into the Valkyrie and the witch shrieked as the vortex began to crumple and the blood dropped to the rocks, covering them both in gore. Morgan wrestled with the woman, and the golden Eye slipped from the Valkyrie's grasp into the gap between the ocean walls, the golden light somehow holding the waves back.

"No," the Valkyrie cried, scrambling away from Morgan, still grasping the staff. The witch leaped from the rocks down into the gap of the ocean. Morgan didn't hesitate, jumping after her and knocking the woman to the ground. Above them, the walls of water loomed, the edges faltered as the power of the light pulsed in and out. The witch scrambled for the Eye of Odin, and Morgan grabbed for the staff, pulling it from the woman's grip, the iron hot in her hands. She felt the spray from the ocean around her, the droplets thicker than the rain, power on the edge of collapse.

Morgan turned and ran, clutching the staff to her as the Valkyrie laid hands on the golden Eye, screaming Norse curses, but the power had gone from the gem. Morgan leaped from the exposed sand as the walls of water came crashing down, the cries of the Valkyrie buried under the boiling ocean. Morgan looked out to the sea as the thunder rolled further off, and the lightning lessened. In the distance, she thought she saw the coils of an ancient creature rise once more and then sink below the depths.

CHAPTER 12

THE NEXT DAY, MORGAN stood at the window in Director Marietti's office, looking out over the tourists in Trafalgar Square as he wound up his phone call. This was the public section of ARKANE, where meetings with outsiders happened, but most of the complex lay under the Square, people walking above, unaware of the secrets kept below. It was a long way from the Bay at the Back of the Ocean and what Morgan had seen in the whirling vortex of blood and boiling waves. The Valkyrie's body had been found washed up on the beach at dawn, her hair bleached completely white, her face frozen in a rictus of horror. Had she glimpsed the realm of Ragnarok at the end, Morgan wondered? Had she seen the warriors waiting to storm back onto the earth for the final battle?

ARKANE had a team of divers searching for the Eye of Odin beneath the waves of the rocky headland. It was dangerous work, hampered by wild ocean currents and inclement weather, and they might never recover it. Perhaps it was better that way.

Marietti put down the phone, turning with a worried expression. He stroked his short gray beard, shot through with white to match his salt-and-pepper hair.

"Martin has traced the funding for the helicopter and

the Neo-Vikings' organization to a front of companies. Behind them sits a group called Tempest." Marietti frowned. "They're new to us, Morgan, but they worry me. The tempest represents upheaval and chaos, a force of nature that can't be stopped. I fear we haven't seen the last of this group."

Morgan heard the words of the Valkyrie in her head, *a storm is coming*, and knew that this was just the beginning.

"I'll have Martin start to research them," Marietti said. "I know you want to work on the package sent from your father next." He picked up the iron staff from the desk, the dull metal giving no sign of the havoc it could wreak when wielded by the right hands. "This will have to go down in the vaults. It can't go back to the British Museum now. Can you explain?"

Morgan nodded. "Of course. There's someone I need to see over there anyway."

***

Crowds outside the British Museum took pictures of the giant cranes repairing the glass roof. The national treasure would be open to the public again soon, and the news reports had inevitably moved onto the next disaster. The Neo-Vikings had been dismissed as a crazy religious group, and any murmurings of the supernatural had been quashed with evidence that the videos of the vortex had been tampered with. No hint of what had occurred on Iona had reached the mainstream news, and ARKANE would make sure it never would.

"Morgan, I'm so glad you could come." Morgan turned to see Blake standing by a coffee cart, two steaming cups in his hands. "I took the liberty …" He raised one of the cups.

She took it smiling, checking the dark liquid inside before taking a sip.

"Just how I like it," Morgan said, wondering if Blake had read something of her in their brief time together, and whether that would be an altogether bad thing.

The cut on the side of his face was a raw pink, the eye socket swollen and bruised in a palette of purple. The color against his darker skin only served to emphasize his piercing blue eyes, and Morgan wondered if this man ever looked really rough. They sat on the low stone wall as tourists milled around them and the hammer of construction rang throughout the square.

"Your curator friend is avenged," Morgan said. "But I'm afraid the museum won't be getting the staff of Skara Brae back."

Blake sighed. "Probably for the best. I'm not sure people here want to remember, anyway." He turned to look into her eyes, searching for the truth. "Did you see what it could do on Iona?"

In a flash of memory, Morgan saw the Valkyrie, floating within the spinning wall of blood, the ray of gold summoning something from the depths. Part of her wanted to share that with Blake. If he touched the staff and read it with his gift, he would see it, too. But he was not ARKANE, and it was time she returned to working with her own team.

"I saw nothing more than we both witnessed here," Morgan said, watching disappointment cloud his eyes. "But the Neo-Vikings won't be back, for sure."

"And will I see you again?" Blake reached for her hand with his gloved one.

Morgan squeezed it as she stood up. "I never say goodbye." She smiled. "I've found that life has too many surprises in store."

She walked away without looking back into the tourist throng, just another face in the crowd.

***

Morgan's adventures continue with the ARKANE team in *Gates of Hell*.

You can find Blake Daniel alongside Detective Jamie Brooke in the London Crime Thrillers.

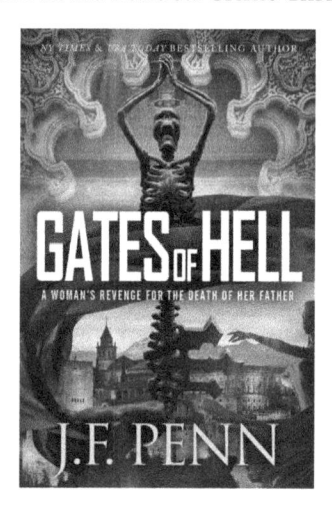

An ancient manuscript that leads to the Gates of Hell.
A woman's revenge for the death of her father.

When the last of the Remnant is murdered at the Sagrada Familia in Barcelona, ARKANE agent Dr Morgan Sierra is drawn into the hunt for a supernatural Key. She's joined by agent Jake Timber, who must face his own fears as they decipher clues left behind by Kabbalist scholars.

From ancient sites in Spain, to Israel and the Czech Republic, Morgan and Jake must follow the trail to the Key, while evading Adam Kadmon, a man consumed with a lust for dark power.

As the planets align, Morgan and Jake race against time to find the Key and destroy it before the Devourers and the Polluted of God emerge from the Gates of Hell to ravage the earth.

ENJOYED DAY OF THE VIKINGS?

If you loved the book and have a moment to spare, I would really appreciate a short review on the page where you bought the book. Your help in spreading the word is gratefully appreciated and reviews make a huge difference to helping new readers find the series. Thank you!

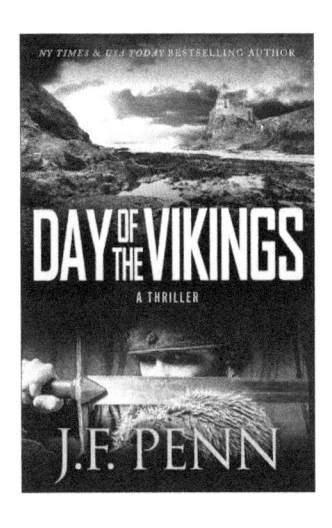

Get a free copy of the bestselling thriller, *Day of the Vikings*, ARKANE book 5, when you sign up to join my Reader's Group. You'll also be notified of new releases, giveaways and receive personal updates from behind the scenes of my thrillers.

WWW.JFPENN.COM/FREE

* * *

Day of the Vikings, an ARKANE thriller

A ritual murder on a remote island under the shifting skies of the aurora borealis.

A staff of power that can summon Ragnarok, the Viking apocalypse.

When Neo-Viking terrorists invade the British Museum in London to reclaim the staff of Skara Brae, ARKANE agent Dr. Morgan Sierra is trapped in the building along with hostages under mortal threat.

As the slaughter begins, Morgan works alongside psychic Blake Daniel to discern the past of the staff, dating back to islands invaded by the Vikings generations ago.

Can Morgan and Blake uncover the truth before Ragnarok is unleashed, consuming all in its wake?

Day of the Vikings is a fast-paced, supernatural thriller set in London and the islands of Orkney, Lindisfarne and Iona. Set in the present day, it resonates with the history and myth of the Vikings.

If you love an action-packed thriller,
you can get Day of the Vikings for free now:

WWW.JFPENN.COM/FREE

Day of the Vikings features Dr. Morgan Sierra from the ARKANE thrillers, and Blake Daniel from the London Crime Thrillers, but it is also a stand-alone novella that can be read and enjoyed separately.

AUTHOR'S NOTE

THIS NOVELLA IS MEANT to be a rollicking fun read! Although I did research the Vikings, this is a work of fiction and I have embellished for dramatic license. The Norse quotes are from the Poetic Edda poem *Völuspá*, where a *völva*, a witch or shaman, tells Odin the story of the creation of the world. You will find the places, manuscripts and objects in 'real' life, but I have turned them into a story of my own construction. All mistakes in research are my own.

You can see associated pictures on Pinterest:
www.pinterest.com/jfpenn/ragnarok

Inspiration for the story

My own fascination with *Game of Thrones* and its Viking mythology of wolves, ravens and dragons first inspired this story. Couple that with the Northern Lights being seen across the UK early in 2014 (http://bit.ly/1jsqbtE) and the Viking Ragnarok proclaimed for Feb 2014 (http://dailym.

ai/1aTiTXq) and I had an inkling for the story I would write.

The British Museum had a special exhibition about the Vikings, which I attended in early March 2014. The longboat and decapitated skeletons were there, as were the other objects described. I love the supernatural so I was struck by the staffs of the *völva* and the information on Viking magic. As I started to research afterwards, I discovered the Poetic Edda and the story took shape.

The British Museum also features in my book *Prophecy*, which was based on an exhibition on religious relics. I foresee many more exhibitions there forming an integral part of my work! I've used artistic license for the floor plan and the exits.

Orkney

The Ring of Brodgar is within the Neolithic heritage site in the Orkney Islands in the far north of Scotland, closer to Norway than London. You can see the aurora borealis there in the winter months.

Lindisfarne

The Viking raid of Lindisfarne is a historical fact. *The Anglo-Saxon Chronicle* records:

"In this year fierce, foreboding omens came over the land of the Northumbrians, and the wretched people shook; there were excessive whirlwinds, lightning, and fiery dragons were seen flying in the sky. These signs were followed by great famine, and a little after those, that same year on 6th ides of January, the ravaging of wretched heathen people destroyed God's church at Lindisfarne."

The Lindisfarne Gospels are in the British Library and can be visited there when not 'resting.' The location of the relics of St Cuthbert are a secret known only to a few monks, although the records show it as intact when the Vikings raided, so my use in pagan ritual is fictionalized. You can look at the Gospels online here: http://www.bl.uk/onlinegallery/sacredtexts/lindisfarne.html. The colophon in the back page of the Gospels is actually a list of who contributed to the creation of the book, but perhaps my version is more interesting!

Iona

The description of Iona is as exact as possible, and its early importance to Christianity is fact.

MORE BOOKS BY J.F.PENN

Thanks for joining Morgan, Jake and the **ARKANE** team. The adventures continue …

Stone of Fire #1
Crypt of Bone #2
Ark of Blood #3
One Day in Budapest #4
Day of the Vikings #5
Gates of Hell #6
One Day in New York #7
Destroyer of Worlds #8
End of Days #9
Valley of Dry Bones #10

If you like **crime thrillers with an edge of the supernatural**, join Detective Jamie Brooke and museum researcher Blake Daniel, in the London Crime Thriller trilogy:

Desecration #1
Delirium #2
Deviance #3

If you enjoy **dark fantasy,** check out:

Map of Shadows, Mapwalkers #1
Risen Gods
American Demon Hunters: Sacrifice

A Thousand Fiendish Angels:
Short stories based on Dante's Inferno

The Dark Queen

More books coming soon.

You can sign up to be notified of new releases, giveaways and pre-release specials - plus, get a free book!

WWW.JFPENN.COM/FREE

ABOUT J.F.PENN

J.F.Penn is the Award-nominated, New York Times and USA Today bestselling author of the ARKANE supernatural thrillers, London Crime Thrillers, and the Mapwalker dark fantasy series, as well as other standalone stories.

Her books weave together ancient artifacts, relics of power, international locations and adventure with an edge of the supernatural. Joanna lives in Bath, England and enjoys a nice G&T.

* * *

You can sign up for a free thriller,
Day of the Vikings, and updates from behind the scenes, research, and giveaways at:

WWW.JFPENN.COM/FREE

* * *

Connect at:
www.JFPenn.com
joanna@JFPenn.com
www.Facebook.com/JFPennAuthor
www.Instagram.com/JFPennAuthor
www.Twitter.com/JFPennWriter

***

For writers:

Joanna's site, www.TheCreativePenn.com, helps people write, publish and market their books through articles, audio, video and online courses.

She writes non-fiction for authors under Joanna Penn and has an award-nominated podcast for writers, The Creative Penn Podcast.

ACKNOWLEDGMENTS

To my readers, thank you so much of your continued support. I hope to keep entertaining you for many years to come.

Thanks to the British Museum for the Viking exhibition, and for all the ideas I continue to have within those hallowed walls.

Thanks to Matt Prior and Joseph Keith Hannaby for providing the practicalities of a helicopter winch through the British Museum's roof. It can be done apparently!

Thanks to Jen Blood, my editor, for her fantastic work in improving the text, and to Wendy Janes for proof-reading so well.

Thanks to Derek Murphy from Creativindie for the brilliant book cover design, and to Jane Dixon Smith at JDSmith Design for the print interior.

Lightning Source UK Ltd.
Milton Keynes UK
UKHW040232121020
371334UK00022B/186